Prai:

Shakespea

"Lively, funny, and agreeably gory."　　　—The Fright Site

"Laugh-out-loud moments! . . . The book is shameless fun, with a decent grounding in the Bard's work."

—*Kirkus Reviews*

"The legend of Shakespeare will never be the same. It's a fun read set against the streets of Elizabethan London."

—*RT Book Reviews*

"Handeland blends Elizabethan and contemporary language skillfully . . . the romance sizzles between the intriguing leads."

—*Publishers Weekly*

"*Shakespeare Undead* is one of the funniest, most action-packed, romantic vampire thrillers I have ever read. This book is certain to join the ranks of great paranormal fiction such as *Twilight* and *Pride and Prejudice and Zombies*. Move over, Edward and Jacob, nothing's sexier than a vampire who knows how to handle a pen."

—*Night Owl Reviews* (Reviewer Top Pick)

Also by Lori Handeland

Zombie Island

A Shakespeare Undead Novel

Lori Handeland

St. Martin's Griffin ☙ New York

ZOMBIE ISLAND. Copyright © 2012 by Lori Handeland. All rights reserved. Printed in the United States of America. For information, address St. Martin's Press, 175 Fifth Avenue, New York, N.Y. 10010.

www.stmartins.com

ISBN 978-0-312-62306-7 (trade paperback)
e-ISBN 978-1-250-01462-7

First Edition: May 2012

10 9 8 7 6 5 4 3 2 1

Zombie Island

Chapter One

"A contract of true love to celebrate."

—*The Tempest* (Act IV, scene I)

London, Autumn—1592

"Two households," murmured William Shakespeare, his gaze fixed on the family crypt of one of them. "In fair London, where we make our scene."

The remains of the day were overcast, as 'twas often the case in fair London. A light rain had begun to tumble down. The dreariness of the weather fit the setting—a shadowy graveyard at dusk, the skies fair weeping over the young mistress so recently entombed.

Will's mistress. The only woman he'd ever loved in several lifetimes.

Will was a vampire, had been for so long he could barely recall when he wasn't. He *wished* that he weren't, that he could live—*really* live—a true lifetime with his love, that he could once again be human; but as far as Will knew, a vampire was forever.

Unless someone cleaved his head or shoved him into the bright morning sun.

"From ancient grudge break to new mutiny," he whispered.

If Kate's husband found out what they had done, his grudge would certainly break something.

"A pair of star-crossed lovers," Will continued, the beginnings of a play he'd been toying with trickling through his mind. A prologue, mayhap, shared by the Chorus, setting up the entire sorry mess he envisioned. He hadn't written a decent tragedy in a while. It was time.

"Whose misadventured piteous overthrows do with their death bury strife."

Only Kate's "death" could bury the strife with her husband. If everything went according to plan—Kate took the potion that made her "appear like death"—then Reginald should have forgotten about his wife the instant the door slammed shut on her tomb. It wasn't as if he loved her. With any luck he would have returned to the New World, and the plantation he managed there for Kate's father, on the next ship, never to be seen or heard from again.

Which would save Will the trouble of killing him.

Just the thought of how the bastard had ill-treated his wife—Will's love—had Will's teeth itching, growing.

"Puppies," he murmured, forcing his mind away from bloody murder. Instead he focused on sweet, fat-bellied balls of fur gamboling across spring grass until his fangs went away.

Will glanced at the azure sky. Now that the sun slept and the moon had awoke, the chill of a London autumn eve would soon seep into the stone mausoleum. Will had promised he would be there to greet Kate when she arose from her feigned death, so he hurried forth, intent on the door beneath the stone-cut lettering.

Dymond.

That was not his love's true name, but she was a fine jewel just the same.

He reached for the door, and the portal swung open of its own accord, emitting a loud, wretched creak that caused Will to start and draw back his hand to rest atop his sword.

He'd come directly from a performance at the Rose Theater still wearing the costume of Valentine—a doublet of dark green wool with breeches a shade lighter. As Valentine becomes king of a band of outlaws, the sword was part of the show.

And proved a welcome adornment when the zombie loomed from the crypt.

"Brrrr!" it said. "Brrrrrrr!"

"Zounds." Will drew his weapon, the slick slide of the metal from its scabbard slicing through the heretofore silent night.

He had not expected zombies. He'd believed London cleared of them by both his efforts and Kate's. That a woman could be an accomplished zombie hunter had at first surprised, then amazed, Will. Together they had fought the lurching horde set upon their queen by one who would topple her throne and throw England into chaos. They had triumphed, but apparently at least one of the creatures had escaped.

Will would have cleaved the horror's head from its shoulders, returning the soul to God and the body to ashes, if he hadn't caught his foot on a loose stone.

There were times when he was grace personified . . .

Will landed on his arse with a thud.

And times when he was not.

The zombie, a well-to-do merchant from the appearance of what was left of his clothes, which hung in tatters and revealed more than Will ever wanted to see of another man's— be he dead or living dead—anatomy, blinked at the sudden disappearance of his prey. One of his eyelids came off, skating down his rotting cheek like parchment skipping off the edge of a tabletop in the wind. The bit of flesh landed on Will's upturned face, and he panicked.

He hacked at the man's legs, but the blows did no harm. The creature merely stepped out of Will's reach and disappeared into the darkened crypt.

Will frowned. Why on earth would the zombie go in there when there were fresh brains to be had right here in Will's head?

Will might be undead, but his brains still worked—quite well, if his reviews were any indication—and they were therefore a delectable meal for any shambling cretin.

Climbing to his feet, Will kept a firm hand on his weapon as he awaited the return of the creature, but the gaping, gloomy doorway remained empty.

"Thou detestable maw." Will crept closer. "Thou womb of death. Gorged with the dearest morsel of the earth."

A chill went over him as he heard his words and understood why the zombie had gone in rather than stay out.

Certainly most of the occupants were long dead, their brains as rotted as the one who now walked among them. But there was one who had not begun to rot. One who lay alone and vulnerable, whose fresh and tasty brains would be a dear morsel for this gibbering fiend.

Will plunged inside, sword at the ready, just in time to see the decaying head haloed in a beam of moonlight as he bent over what had to be the resting place of Will's sweet love.

"Brr!" the creature said again. "Brrrr."

In truth, zombies rarely said aught else.

Leaping forward, Will sliced through its neck with one

sweep of his blade. The zombie disintegrated, coating Will's face with ash.

"Zombies," he muttered, wiping the gritty remnants from his eyes. "I *hate* those guys."

An image flickered—a man in a battered brown hat sneering at other men in pressed uniforms as they goose-stepped past, arms stretched upward in a salute.

An invincible hero. The ultimate evil.

Will shook his head, and the idea disappeared. He tried very hard to bring it back.

"Something about an ark," he murmured, but it was gone, driven from his mind by more pressing matters.

Will tightened his fingers about the hilt of his sword, gaze scanning the crypt for anything that moved. But the tomb remained as still as those who inhabited it.

He moved to the flat stone pallet where Kate should rest. Nothing was there.

Desperately, Will searched every crevice and corner. He found dozens of bodies in as many states of rot, but not a single trace of Kate.

Why was he surprised?

The course of true love never did run smooth.

Chapter Two

"I would fain die a dry death."

—*The Tempest* (Act I, scene I)

I awoke to a darkness so great it seemed to pulse.

Nay! To rock.

For an instant I could not recall what had happened before I'd gone to sleep. But a memory such as that would not stay silent for long. Will's voice, as he laid out the plan, drifted through my mind.

Tomorrow night be certain to lie alone. Of this distilled liquor drink. Through your veins shall run a cold and drowsy humor. Your pulse will cease.

I had drunk of the liquor, and from that moment on I remembered naught.

And in this borrowed likeness of death you will continue two-and-forty hours, then awake as from a pleasant sleep.

I should now repose within the Dymond family crypt. And Will should be here. He had promised.

I will come and watch you wake and we will away. This, sweet Kate, will free us from our present trouble.

I did not feel free from trouble. I felt, instead, in the thick of it. Such was the story of my life.

I am a *chasseur*, a hunter. For years I have stalked those whose souls are controlled by another. I call them the *tibonage*. You'd call them zombies.

They're everywhere.

Because of them I'd met William Shakespeare. Mistaking him for a zombie, I'd nearly lopped off his head. Thank goodness I'd missed. That head, and what lay in it, was far too brilliant to disappear from this world.

I tried to sit up and encountered resistance. From what, I could not see. I had never been in a place so dark in all my life.

Perhaps I *had* died. But if so—

My indrawn breath seemed overly loud, as if the sound had gone forth and been thrust back. As if I were confined in a very small space.

I could not be a zombie. They had no thoughts. Their brains were gruel. They said little beyond "Brrr!" unable, even, to articulate completely what they sought.

"Brains," I said distinctly. "And I feel no burning urge to partake of any." Forsooth, the idea sent a wave of nausea through me. Therefore I was not a zombie.

But I *was* confined and I needed, desperately, to be free.

I was also surrounded by small hard lumps of something, which rattled when I moved and gave off the scent of a long dead fire. When I extended my right hand the articles parted, and my fingers met wood; to the left I encountered the same. I stretched my toes and tapped another board.

"God's kneecaps!" I knew a coffin when I felt one.

Why was I not interred upon a bier in the Dymond family crypt?

Family crypts were unusual in England, where the poor still went into the ground and the rich often bought a section of the local church or monastery to serve as their mausoleum. To have one's own tomb was immodest. Even the once Bluff King Hal was buried in St. George's Chapel, along with dozens of other royal corpses.

However, of late, anything Italian was the rage. It seemed that every fool in London walked around with an Italian rapier strapped to his waist. My husband had taken the Italian fascination a step further and purchased an ancient vault to use in the Italian manner for a private family tomb. He'd even ordered what Dymond remains that remained moved into it.

So why wasn't I there?

Had Reginald tossed me into a box and buried me in the garden? Considering what I knew of my husband, such behavior would not surprise me.

To be fair, I had not been the best of wives. But I could not help it. I would love Will Shakespeare unto the end of my days. Which, at the moment, did not appear to number all that many.

Closing my eyes, I attempted to still my racing heart, my overwrought breathing, and listened. Not only was I rocking, but in the distance I heard—

My eyes snapped open. "Water."

Instead of stuffing me into the family crypt then hying himself back to the New World, Reginald had brought me along. Considering he believed me a rotting corpse, such behavior was more disturbing than any of his behavior thus far.

Although it did explain the small hard items that surrounded me. Corpses were often packed in charcoal to prevent decay when they had to be moved a long distance.

I bit my lip and considered. I could not remain in this box until we reached the Virginia shore. If I did so, I'd be as dead as Reginald thought me.

But if I escaped, what then? My husband could not see me alive or our entire plot would unravel. I must be free of him, and he would do well to be free of me. Reginald wanted wealth, a title, and an heir. All I wanted was Will.

We had come together but a few weeks past—a zombie hunter and the vampire with the ability to raise them, a wealthy, married woman and a playwright. In truth we would not have met if I had not been trolling the night with my sword. But once met, we could not seem to remain apart.

I had despaired of love, but I had found it in him, and once touched, once kissed, once loved, we could not bear a life without the other in it. So we had contrived to change things.

I brushed my fingertips across one wall of my coffin. This was the result. Mayhap I deserved worse for my perfidy, but I had discovered that without love I did not want to live.

And so, I had "died."

Determined, I clenched my fists. I would hide upon the ship, steal food and water. I would stay alive, whatever it took. And hope that when the vessel finished its voyage to the New World, it then returned to the Old.

If only I had my sword. I would make short work of this box. However, when I felt about some more, I encountered only splinters and the skirt of my very best gown. But the farthingale that kept the garment bell-shaped was missing, along with the painful body-stitchets to hasp my waist as well as the usual annoying array of petticoats. From what I could gather, I wore only my gown and a chemise.

In your best robes on the bier you will be borne to the same ancient vault where all the Dymonds lie.

Will had been nearly right. I wore my best robes, but the bier had borne me to a ship and not the vault.

Poor Will! What must he have thought when he opened the crypt and found me absent?

Our plan had been for him to sit by my side as I awakened, then we would away to Bath, where I would tarry a while, a lady partaking of the medicinal waters to soothe her frazzled nerves. By the by I would return to London. With a few changes to my hair, my accent, my clothes, no one would believe the live Kate and the dead Katherine the same woman, and I would at last be liberated. Instead I was a prisoner.

Angry, frustrated, and—I admit it—scared, I kicked both feet.

And felt a slight give in the wooden wall of my tomb.

Again, I kicked. Again, the plank bowed. Encouraged, I continued the proceedings, resting when my legs became tired, ignoring the pain in my bare heels.

Eventually my determination was rewarded with a sharp, welcome *crack,* and the lowermost wall of my coffin tumbled downward, landing upon the heaving floor with a clatter, charcoal pieces thunking like distant, heavy rain.

Without support, the board above me sagged. I lifted my hands and knocked it away too. Seconds later I scrambled free, then stared at what could have been my final resting place.

Though the box had been made for one who should no longer move, let alone kick, I was still amazed at the shoddiness of the workmanship. Did it reflect Reginald's parsimonious nature or merely his opinion of me?

"The wind," came the call from above, "she be backin' into the east!"

"There be spume upon the water," another replied.

"We'd best batten down afore that squall o'ertakes us."

"Aye, Captain!"

"You there! Hie below and make sure her ladyship does not get tossed hither and yon."

It took me several ticks of a clock to realize "her ladyship" was me. I leaped forward, snatching at the fallen timber, putting it back to rights, hoping the contraption would not fall apart the instant it was touched and reveal an empty space. I ducked behind several barrels just in time.

A swarthy, bowlegged seaman negotiated the steps and made his way to the coffin. His gaze cast about, flicking over the barrels where I crouched, coming to rest upon a coil of thick rope nearby. He snatched it and set to wrapping the piece around my empty resting place, first lengthwise, then crosswise. After tugging on the loops, he gave a nod then disappeared topside.

I crept from my hiding place, dizzy with the realization of how narrowly I'd avoided being trapped there. I, too, gave a tug on the seaman's ropes and was satisfied that the ramshackle conveyance would not collapse to reveal the disturbing lack of a body.

Perhaps Reginald would bury this box without ever looking inside, and my "death" would continue unquestioned. Even if he did take a peek within—ghoulish as that might be—I doubted he would consider that I had never been dead in the first place. Most likely he would believe my body lost along the way or stolen by the natives.

My nurse, Nounou, who had taught me of the *tibonage* and trained me as a *chasseur* in her own image, had told tales of Africa, where she had been born, and Haiti, where she had been dragged—both dark, exotic places full of strange practices and stranger beliefs, many of which involved the dead, or what was left of them. It would not be surprising if the New World's brutal native tribes held some of the same beliefs and would be happy to snatch a corpse if the opportunity presented itself.

The ship pitched violently, and a wash of seawater poured through the open trapdoor and splashed over my bare feet. I frowned at my toes, as filthy as the rest of me after being tossed about with hundreds of pieces of coal, then wiggled them a bit. I supposed Reginald had ordered all my velvet slippers sold. Why stick a pair on feet that would only molder? I was surprised he'd bothered to clothe me at all.

Which reminded me—I must find other attire. It would be impossible to sneak about the ship in a golden brocade gown. However, if I was dressed as a boy—something I had done often enough when fighting zombies—I should blend in.

As I turned toward the stairs a waterfall cascaded through the opening, splashing onto the floor then swirling about my ankles and dampening the hem of my skirt.

I shivered at the icy chill. The spurt of voices in the night only caused those shivers to deepen.

"We blew out a sail!"

"Strip her to bare poles!"

"Too late. We are dismasted!"

"We're going down!"

A sickening crack was echoed by thunder. The ship listed. The flow through the opening slowed to a trickle, and I took the opportunity to scramble topside.

All hands occupied with the storm, no one spared me a glance. I nearly went over the edge as the vessel righted herself, sending a sluice of ocean across the bow. I grabbed the nearest solid object, the capstan—a wooden drum attached through the deck, used like a pulley by the crew—and held on as the sky above split open, spilling brilliant white light over us all.

The scene was etched in silver—the height of the waves, the whip of the wind, the violent pitch of the boat, the cracked mast, the missing sail, the desperate scramble of everyone left alive.

I had come so far. I had survived so much. But none of that mattered in the face of the storm.

The deck splintered; the capstan sank, along with everything else. I hit the fiercely foaming water, and then . . .

I knew no more.

Chapter Three

"Misery acquaints a man with strange bed-fellows."
—*The Tempest* (Act II, scene 2)

At a loss, Will slumped upon the cold, hard, empty stone that should have housed his love. What was the last thing Kate had said to him?

It seems the perfect plan. What could go wrong?

Will let out a sharp bark of laughter that did not sound at all amused. "What, indeed?" he murmured. He only wished that he knew.

Kate should have drunk of the elixir Will had purchased from the apothecary. The next morning she would have appeared dead. Her husband should have entombed her. Will should have found her here.

So where was she?

"You must go after de girl."

Will lifted his head so fast the whole world spun. He didn't need to see the brightly adorned Moorish woman who perched on the edge of an already occupied bier to know who it was. Both her accent and her presence here among the dead revealed her identity.

"Nounou." Will leaped to his feet. "Where is she? Where is my sweet Kate?"

"In de hold of a ship named *Anna Gale,* far out upon de sea."

"A ship? But—" Then, suddenly, he knew. "That bastard!"

Nounou's lips curved. "He is dat."

Kate's old, dead nurse had never much cared for Kate's husband. Will would have liked the woman for that alone, but the former *chasseur* had proved invaluable.

Too bad only Will could see and hear her.

He'd been born a necromancer; he had an affinity for the dead. As a child he hadn't realized the people who appeared and disappeared were ghosts, so he'd spoken to them.

Back then, before Britain was a gleam in Caesar's eye, conversing with the dead would get you burned. Will had narrowly avoided such a fate on several occasions.

While becoming undead had solved that concern—mere fire would not kill him—it had brought about others.

One moment he'd been dying of some disease in a hovel, on a hill in the British countryside, the next a man with oddly sharp teeth had appeared at his bedside. He had given Will a choice: Perish or embrace a new life. With stories swirling in his head that had never been put to words, still young with so much yet to do, Will had chosen this.

However, instead of teaching Will how to exist as a creature of the darkness, Will's maker had changed him and moved on, leaving Will to learn about his new un-life on his own.

Trouble had ensued.

Nounou clapped her hands. *"Faites l'attention!"*

"Your pardon," Will begged, returning from past misfortunes to present concerns. "Why would my love's husband bring what he believes is his dead wife along on a ship to the New World?"

"He did not want to leave you even de comfort of her body. No place for you to visit, no place to stand and mourn."

"Ass," Will muttered.

"Oui." Nounou inclined her head, the brightly colored band of cloth that hid her hair emphasizing the movement. "But dere is difficulty ahead. She may yet die."

"Die?" Will repeated. If he'd still possessed a beating heart, he feared it would fair leap from his chest as panic surged.

"No time to explain. You must away. Take passage on de first ship to de New World. Help her." Nounou began to fade. "Save her. You are Kat'erine's only hope."

The old woman disappeared, leaving Will to contemplate the pile of bones she'd been perched upon. As she hadn't really been there except in spirit, the pile remained undisturbed.

Will's hand clenched and unclenched. Having Kate out of his reach, yet in danger, made him feel helpless—one thing he had rarely felt since becoming an immortal vampire. Of course, *Kate* was not immortal. Even though she often behaved as if she were.

When she fought zombies, she did so as if she could never die, throwing herself into the fray with very little concern for her own safety.

Will groaned. No wonder Nounou was worried. Out there in the great, wide, deadly world, without Will to watch her back, anything could happen.

Suddenly Nounou's mouth appeared, hovering in the air directly in front of Will's face. Nothing else—no head, no eyes, no body—just lips and teeth and tongue.

"Go!" it shouted.

Will went.

He was in luck. A ship would leave for the New World the following morn. Unfortunately, the offered accommodations were unsatisfactory.

"There's room with the men," the captain said. "That's all I 'ave."

"I require my own quarters," Will murmured.

Every day at dawn Will fell into a deathlike sleep. Until the sun reached its peak, nothing on the earth would wake him. This was not something he wanted anyone else to observe. What if they decided to drag him into the newly born sun in order to rouse him?

"The only private quarters are mine," snarled the crusty seaman. "And you ain't gettin' 'em."

Will hated to use his vampire powers on humans. It made him feel brutish and unclean. But sometimes, he just had to.

He stared into the captain's eyes. "I will pay you for the use of your cabin."

Will had funds—living forever had its advantages—he just hadn't been able to use any of them lately. A common playwright with ample coin would raise suspicions.

But no one need know how much he had paid this man. Will wouldn't even *have* to pay him. He could merely tell the captain that he *had* been paid and the man would believe it. However, Will wasn't that kind of vampire.

"You will gladly allow me to occupy your quarters," Will continued, pressing a bag of coins into the fellow's hardened hand.

"Gladly. Aye," the man repeated as if entranced. In truth, he was.

Will possessed the ability to look into the eyes of human

beings and give them a "push" with the power of his mind. They would do whatever he asked, then they would forget.

"No one, not even you, shall step foot into that room on this voyage. Make certain of it."

"Aye," the captain said again. "I will make certain."

When the ship set sail early the next morn, Will lay dead asleep on the captain's pallet. All hands had been warned to steer clear of that cabin, and they would not disobey. The captain had been at sea since he was a boy, and he brooked no disobedience. He preferred his crew fear him rather than love him. He was well aware that mutiny was only one short lull away.

Will slept the sleep of the undead long past the time he usually rose. He might have continued well into the night if he had not suddenly been tossed onto the floor. Without his amazing vampire speed, which caused him to bring up his arms midfall, his nose would have cracked against the floorboards and likely broken.

He could take blood from a seaman—Will's saliva would cure the bite, a little push would eliminate the memory—and heal such an injury, but he preferred not to. Though most vampires considered abstaining from blood a weakness, Will believed it a strength.

In the beginning, the bloodlust was all Will had known. As time passed, he needed blood less and less. Age brought not only wisdom but also an advancement in this species; he could go years without imbibing.

Certainly, there came a time when he must partake, but he always drank the smallest amount necessary to survive, and he told himself that while he might on occasion *need* blood, he did not *want* it.

However, in the darkest hours of the long, long nights, Will knew the truth. He abstained because he feared that if he gave in to those desires, he would never be able to stop. That had nearly been the case with Kate.

"Mine eyes have drawn thy shape," he murmured. If he closed them, he could see her—dark hair, dark gaze, not the fashion for most, but for him— "Delights."

Another sonnet, Will thought, to his Dark Lady. He tried to envision more but could not. He'd discovered, since having found Kate, he could no longer write without her.

Which was reason enough—even if he hadn't been totally besotted—to get her back.

Climbing to his feet, Will threw out his arms to steady himself as the ship pitched and rolled. He had been on ships before—with Caesar to Egypt, with Richard to Burgundy, with Henry VIII to France—and none had ever heaved as violently as this.

Will opened the door, and a blast of foam slapped him in the face. The sun that should be blazing upon gentle blue waters was nowhere in evidence. Neither were the gentle blue waters. Instead an angry black sea roiled beneath clouds the shade of slate.

The captain stood nearby, peering at the ocean below. It was only when Will joined him that he heard the odd clunks and scrapes against the side of the ship. Will, too, peered over the edge. Jagged bits of wood floated on the surface. There and here barrels bobbed.

"Oh, no," Will whispered. Not all of the bobbing dark objects were barrels. Some of them looked like heads.

"Appears this storm was worse afore," the captain said, gaze still on the debris. "Much worse."

"Aye," Will agreed, a distant sort of sadness filling him at the loss of all those souls he did not even know. He liked humans; if he didn't, he would never have sworn off drinking from them.

"Mayhap survivors reached yon island." The captain lifted his roughened hand and pointed an oft broke finger at the horizon. "Though I don't recall there ever being an island there before."

Will's gaze narrowed. The low, blue-black hump in the distance more resembled a monster of the sea than a strip of land, but he supposed the captain knew best.

The man squinted into the dim. "I didn't see it on no charts neither."

A trickle of unease lifted the fine hairs on Will's arms. Why, he wasn't sure. The world was a wonder. There were so many things of which humans were unaware. Things that would never, ever appear on a chart.

"We'll advance," the captain decided. "'Tis best to look and see."

Will opened his mouth to argue—he did not want to fall too far behind Kate—then snapped it shut again as he caught sight of something in the water that made his already cold blood run ever colder.

A broken board with two words writ upon it.

Anna Gale.

Will stopped breathing. Not that he needed to breathe; he did so only to appear human. Nevertheless, his chest began to ache.

Kate could not be dead. He would not *let* her be dead.

Except if she already was . . .

Will watched the bit of board that read *Anna Gale* swirl away. He had to find out.

"Yes," Will agreed in a voice that sounded as lifeless as he feared his love to be. "Let us look and see."

"Too late," the captain whispered.

The storm uncoiled from the horizon like a dragon from its lair, spitting lightning instead of fire; thunder was its roar. Waterspouts whirled atop the surface of the sea as if the dragon's tail thrashed, poking up in a hundred different directions.

The dragon's name was Tempest, and she was hungry. She bore down on the ship and devoured every living soul within.

Chapter Four

" 'Tis far off, and rather like a dream than an assurance."

—*The Tempest* (Act I, scene 2)

I awoke to a dazzling night sky. Stars so plentiful and bright they hurt my eyes, the half-moon so white it seemed to pulse.

Shifting, I moaned as aches shot through my body. I smelled like a fish market, and when I lifted my hand seaweed trailed from my thumb.

I turned my head toward the sea. Nothing bobbed there but the reflection of the moon.

I sat up. I was alone on a beach framed by empty ocean and enough dense foliage to be a jungle. Considering Will's assurance that the distilled liquor I had drunk would cause me to be in the likeness of death for two-and-forty hours, we could not have been more than a day out of port when the storm hit. We'd been nowhere near temperate waters.

Though I had been soaked by an ocean that should be quite chill, I did not shiver. The balmy breeze that fluttered across the greenery instead felt heavenly warm.

Perhaps I *was* in heaven. That would explain much.

For instance, how I'd gotten here since by all rights I should have sunk like an anchor the instant I went into the water. Even if I had known how to swim, the heavy brocade of my skirts would have pulled me swiftly to rest at the bottom of the sea. Then there was the fact that an isle of such temperate climes could not possibly exist in the southwest approach.

On the other hand . . . I was a zombie hunter in love with a vampire. Impossible meant very little any longer.

Still . . . Where were all the others? I could not be the only one to have survived. At the least there should be bodies.

Which brought me round again to the question of heaven. However, would heaven be empty but for me?

"Purgatory," I whispered.

Though the old faith had gone the way of Bloody Queen Mary and England was considered now a Protestant country— we had to be, as Queen Elizabeth's birth had been made legitimate by her father's break with Rome—Henry VIII's religion was at times more Catholic than Catholic.

According to church teachings, purgatory was a place reserved for the purification of those not yet ready to enter heaven. Considering my adulterous behavior with what most would label a "demon," not to mention my unwomanly zombie hunting and the huge lie that was my death—or at least the lie it had been until my drowning—I should not be surprised to find myself there.

Except this place was more paradise than purgatory.

Unknown trees towered above leafy fronds of equally unfamiliar origin. All were luscious and full; the remnants of the rain still shimmered upon them.

A seemingly endless range of green astounded me—from the shade of a fog hovering over a spring meadow to a thick, deep emerald. Yet dotted haphazardly about was an array of flowers of such astonishing jewel-toned brilliance I could not believe they were real.

The ocean, now calm, ebbed to and fro, near lulling me to sleep. The breeze, a warm caress, carried the scent of sun and leaves and life. How could I possibly be dead?

"Are you my diamond?"

I gasped as the sweet, high-pitched voice seemed to pour from the air. I peered here, then there, but I was still as alone as I'd been all along.

"How now?" I called. "Come forth. Show yourself."

"Are you?" the voice repeated, then before I could answer continued, "But you must be. Only the diamond could survive my promised storm."

"*Your* storm?"

"My master ordered me to bring the tempest, and I did."

"Who is your master?" I climbed to my feet. I certainly hoped she didn't say Beelzebub. I hadn't been that wicked, had I?

"No time for talk. Remove your gown."

"I think not." Though the voice sounded female, that did not mean I would disrobe in front of it.

"'Twill be a hindrance. You, of all people, should know this."

My gown *was* a ruin—blackened by the charcoal, torn, soaked—it weighed heavily upon me. But what possible difference could that make now?

"Who are you?" I asked. "Why can't I see you?"

"I am Ariel, a magical sprite. I have power over the wind and the water."

I wanted to scoff. Sprites, magic, controlling of the wind and water. Insanity! But, as previously mentioned, a zombie hunter had no business mocking anything.

"How came I here?" I asked.

"I cast a spell to save the diamond."

"I'm not a diamond. That is merely my name." And one I would much rather not claim. "I am Katherine Dymond. With a 'y.'"

"There is nothing mere about you, *chasseur.*"

I stilled, face canted toward the air from whence poured the voice. "How do you know that?"

"A sprite knows many things, and how she knows matters not. What matters is I saved you from the deep."

"Then I'm not dead?"

A trill of laughter danced among the stars. "My spells never fail. I wanted to save the diamond, and save you I did."

I wasn't sure what to say beyond "Thank you."

"I doubt you will thank me for this."

Of a sudden, my heavy, stinking skirt was wrenched away.

"Halt!" I cried, even though I was glad to see the garment go. The air sifting through the thin chemise, which was all that now covered my legs, felt divine.

Ariel did not halt; instead the sleeves were ripped away, leaving my arms bare to the gentle night. Without them the bodice, torn down the center in my unremembered struggles with the sea, slid off.

The shriek of rending cloth continued. The sudden increase of air against my limbs as the tattered chemise below my knees—for some reason, Reginald had buried me in undergarments meant for the ragbag—tore away, should have made me cry out. Instead, I sighed with pleasure at the unexpected freedom.

"Hark! They come."

"They?" A thousand ants seem to run along my neck. I even slapped at the itch, but nothing was there. "Who are they?"

A sword dropped from the sky, landing at my feet with a tinny *clunk*.

"Welcome," Ariel said, "to Zombie Island."

Chapter Five

"The devil speaks in him."

—*The Tempest* (Act V, scene 1)

Reginald Dymond awoke feeling as if he'd eaten sand for supper then washed it down with half the ocean.

His head throbbed; he couldn't move without moaning, and even his eyelids hurt when he attempted to open them.

"Arthur!" he croaked, calling for his manservant.

The only thing that answered was the breeze.

"Nurse!" he tried next. But even if she had been near, she had grown too deaf to hear anything less powerful than a bellow years ago.

"Kath—" he began, then everything came back. His treacherous wife was dead.

Reginald's lips curved as he recalled ordering her body placed in the hold of his ship. He planned to bury her in Virginia, out where the savages roamed. Perhaps they'd even dig her up and shove some of her bones through their noses. He quite liked the idea of her spending eternity showered with the snot of a wild Indian.

'Twas no less than she deserved for cuckolding him with a

common playwright. At the least, removing her from England would keep her lover from haunting her burial place. All Reginald would need to complete his utter mortification was for that ass William Shakespeare to write a sonnet to his dead love. The work would no doubt become a rousing success, and people would be standing outside the Dymond family crypt wailing as they read the beauteous words and feeling sorry for a dead adulterous bitch. Reginald would never get rid of them, or the stigma of being the one she had betrayed.

As it was, he'd had to hie aboard the first available ship and return posthaste to the vile shores of the New World, lest the queen discover his wife's untimely demise so soon after the old crone had cautioned Reginald not to harm her.

He hadn't. He wasn't stupid; Queen Elizabeth had just bestowed upon him a barony. Not out of the goodness of her heart, of course, but out of the parsimoniousness of her purse. Katherine's father had paid her well for it.

One of the reasons Reginald had married Katherine—mayhap the only reason, or at least the best—was her father's promise to buy Reginald a title once a profit was made on the tobacco plantation he'd been given charge of in the New World.

Queen Elizabeth was not only her father's daughter in many ways but also her grandfather's granddaughter, and Henry VII had known how to squeeze a coin until it screamed. That the queen shared this trait might be why England was once again a wealthy country, even after the ravages of Queen Mary and her advisers.

Nevertheless, Reginald found his monarch's tendency to avarice galling. Not that he'd ever say so.

Though his eyes seemed stuck together, Reginald set his teeth, wincing at the grit that crunched between them, and forced his lids to open. Then he howled in pain as sand coated his eyeballs. He lifted his hands, attempted to rub away the granules that felt like glass grating upon him, and only served in scratching his skin as his fingers were likewise coated.

Where was he? What had happened?

He crawled about on all fours; tears streamed down his face. Panic caused his breathing to increase; the harshness of his pants only served to upset him further.

"Arthur!" he howled.

Once again, his only answer was the wind.

And the water. He turned his maligned visage toward the rolling lap of the waves then scrambled in that direction until warm liquid washed over his fingers.

Eagerly he splashed his face then took a large mouthful in hopes of washing the grit from his mouth. He spat the brine away and wailed some more as the filth fell upon his arms and chest and chin.

"How now!" said a deep, commanding voice. "Cease that horrendous squalling. You sound like a mad beast."

"Who goes there?" Reginald demanded. Then, feeling at a disadvantage, he clambered from all fours onto two feet.

He swiped impatiently at his face and opened his eyes, thrilled to discover the tears had washed away much of the sand. They still stung, and he would have liked nothing better than to shut them again and sink down until one of his servants came to bathe him. But the sight that greeted him made Reginald forget, for a moment, his current woes.

A large, imposing fellow in tattered robes, clutching an ancient tome as if it were gold, emerged from the thick foliage. For an instant, Reginald gaped at the jungle, the beach, the clear starry night. Then the man reached him, and his brilliant blue eyes seemed to bore into Reginald's own pale reflections like fire.

"How came you here?" the chap demanded.

"How came *you* here?" Reginald returned.

He was a *baron*. *He* asked the questions. For instance—

"Where is here?"

The man, whose long, tangled red-and-white hair blew in the breeze like a standard, scowled. "You are on *my* island, boy. And, breathing, you do not belong."

"Breathing?" Reginald repeated, confused. Why wouldn't he be breathing?

"How did you survive the shipwreck? The storm?"

At the stranger's words, everything came back in a rush that tore through Reginald's mind so fast he nearly swooned.

The ship. The storm. His terror as the two collided.

The shouts. The screams—mostly his—the chill of the water as it closed over his head. Then . . . nothing.

Until he'd woken here.

"I suppose you rescued me." Reginald sighed. "And now you want a reward."

The fellow's lip curled back, but instead of answering, he shouted, "Ariel! Come to me, sprite, and be quick."

Was the chap mad? He behaved so, striding back and forth across the sand, bellowing to the steadily lightening sky for his "slave," his "fairy," his "magician," to appear.

"Thou shouldst lie down and rest," Reginald said.

This man must have been on the ship too, though Reginald had not seen him. Through a great miracle, they had reached land, but his companion's head had run afoul of a board, a barrel, a ballast, and he had lost his sense.

Reginald had no time to spare for a lunatic. He needed to

discover where he was, what had happened, and how soon and how much it would cost to be on his way.

"Sirrah!" He snatched the old fellow's elbow, only to have it ripped from his grasp as the other turned on him, gaze so wide the whites of his eyes blazed in the waning light of the moon and his wild hair floated about his head like a crown.

"Sirrah, you say? As if I were a lesser man than thee? Who dost though think thou art?" He looked Reginald up and down with a contemptuous sneer.

Reginald, long poor and never handsome, had seen such sneers before. They'd always infuriated him. Then, he'd had no recourse. Now, he was a wealthy man and of the peerage.

"You may address me as 'my lord.'" Reginald sniffed, the sound quite loud, but he could not help it considering the size of his nose. That nose had forever been his curse, as it not only was large but also sported a hairy mole upon the end.

His hair was fashionably pale, although there was precious little of it, his eyes a faded blue. However, he'd never had good sight and most did not notice their summer sky shade because he often had to squint in order to see farther than the end of his arm.

At least he was tall and not prone to fat, even before he'd been banished to the other side of the sea, where edible food appeared on his table so rarely as to be nigh on to a miracle.

"My lord?" the old man shouted. "My lord?"

"Aye," Reginald agreed. "It is the way you should address your betters."

He thought then that his companion might have a fit of apoplexy; his face turned bright red. Again Reginald reached for his arm; he would force the old fellow to sit. Again the man jerked it from his grasp.

"You beast," he snapped. "Thou must be an unnatural being, or thou wouldst not breathe." He paused and then began to whisper as if to himself. "Aye. I ordered all men upon the ships to die. If he were human, he would not be walking upon this isle. Therefore, a beast he must be."

The fellow glared at Reginald, who glared right back. A beast? Indeed! How dared he?

"To make certain all who gaze upon him know the low, unholy creature that resides within, I will make his outside resemble his inside." He opened the book and began to page through.

"What nonsense do you spout?" Reginald asked. "Pray cease speaking, rest, before you do yourself some injury."

"Aha!" The man jabbed a crooked finger at an open page, then stabbed it toward Reginald's mole. "Thou poisonous slave, got by the Devil himself. Upon thy wicked dam, come forth!"

"You have gone mad." Reginald took a step backward, concerned no longer that the fool might hurt himself but that he might, instead, hurt Reginald. The stranger was very old, but the mad often possessed the strength of ten.

"I'll rack thee with old cramps." The man stalked forward, keeping pace with Reginald as he stumbled back, glancing down at the book occasionally as if he were reading from it. "Fill all thy bones with aches. Make thee roar. That beasts shall tremble at thy din."

Of a sudden, Reginald's belly cramped. He doubled over, grasping at his middle. His bones did not so much ache as burn. He fell to his knees as insane laughter rang in his suddenly sensitive ears.

"My goblins will grind your joints, with dry convulsions, shorten up your sinews."

As if every word the fellow said were law, Reginald's body

obeyed. His joints ground together so horribly he heard them shriek. He convulsed; his very sinews shortened. His skin was afire; his teeth were in agony. His cursed nose seemed about to explode.

"A caliban you are—half man, half monster." The ancient fool slapped the book closed with a clap loud as thunder. "Behold!"

He pointed to a nearby puddle that had not yet been drawn back to the sea. Reginald crawled there on all fours. After the dry convulsions, he was quite thirsty. However, he never got that drink. For as he leaned over the still, clear water, the moon illuminated his face.

And then . . .

He did roar.

Chapter Six

"The sea cannot drown me."

—*The Tempest* (Act III, scene 2)

Will walked beneath the water. As he did not need to breathe, this did not disturb him in the least. Not as much as what floated above his head.

The bobbing bodies of everyone who had once been aboard his ship.

The storm had dashed the vessel to bits, tossing the crew hither and yon. The screams! The cries! The exhortations to their Lord! At first Will had tried to save a few. But despite his vampire strength, Mother Nature was stronger, and she wanted everyone dead.

The waves tore clinging fingers from Will's over and over again. The seamen would attempt to swim back; Will would attempt to catch up. But before he could reach them, or they him, a wave would dash their heads beneath the surface, and they would not return alive. Eventually, Will could bear no more and let himself sink.

He set a course for the island. If he shuffled his feet as if he were walking, the movement took him in the direction he wished to go. Every so often he kicked to the surface to observe how far he had come. He always emerged right next to a dead body. They were everywhere, and they all seemed to be going where he was.

A deserted beach on a bizarrely temperate isle.

Tired with all these, he thought, *for restful death I cry.*

The only thing that kept him moving forward instead of sinking to the bottom and staying there was the possibility that his sweet Kate might have made it to land ahead of him.

Tired with all these. Will peered at the dozens of bobbing corpses. *From these would I be gone. Save that, to die, I leave my love alone.*

To hope Kate remained alive was foolish. Will had seen nothing but the dead. Even if she had awoken from her slumber, escaped whatever confinement she'd been in, learned magically to swim, the sea had been a tempest. Anyone needing to breathe was lost.

Will stifled a sob. Such would only push seawater into his throat and up his nose. This had happened to him twice already. If he was going to stay undead, and he wasn't yet certain that he would, or could, he preferred to do so without the burning of the salt water inside his nose. When that happened he could not think.

But perhaps he did not want to. He feared if he did, he would think only of his Kate.

Truly dead now, because of him.

In black ink my love may still shine bright.

Oh, shut up! he thought, the words loud in his head, even though, beneath the sea, he could not allow them to come out his mouth.

His mind forever trilled sonnets, snippets of plays, and the like, reminding Will that he had become a vampire for precisely that reason.

He lived for the beauty of words, for the chance to share them with others. He had embraced immortality so that he would have enough time on this earth to set upon the page all the creations that broiled within him.

But he had discovered his muse was Kate. Without her he produced garbage. Certainly the words still came; he doubted they would ever stop. But when they came, they did so in maddeningly small spurts, always a jumble, both too confusing and too inconsequential to be of value. Only when she was at his side did the rush of language and imagery settle into anything of form. What would he do without her?

The urge to sob came again, and this time Will did not think he would be able to stop, so he kicked upward.

His head broke the surface more quickly than it had before. He had nearly reached the island—along with dozens of dead companions.

One of them bobbed against him. "Too late, kind sir, too late," Will murmured, pushing the seaman gently away.

If he'd had more warning, Will could have created others like him—vampires who would have survived the sea. But would he have?

"No," Will murmured.

There was too much to be taken into account, so many things to be lost with only immortality to gain. Will had not known when he had been changed how difficult the centuries to follow would be, how many would die because of him. If he had, would he have chosen death instead?

He wasn't sure. But he had never made another like him without good cause and much consideration. Two things sadly lacking when the tempest came.

Will strode up the beach, then sat beneath a tree and counted the bodies the waves brought in. It kept him from thinking of Kate.

He was interrupted when the air stirred strangely. Intrigued, Will rose as a flicker of sparks shot through the waning night.

A woman took form, silvery as the moon, naked as his soul, her beauty not of this earth. Her feet hovered above the sand, yet Will could see no wings.

"Thou doth suffer a sea-change, into something rich and strange. Sea-nymphs hourly ring thy knell." She sighed, the sound one of the saddest Will had ever known. "Destiny, that instrument of this world and what is in't, hath caused the never-surfeited sea to belch up you. And on this island where man doth not inhabit, you 'mongst men being most unfit to live." She glanced over her shoulder, the movement furtive, then whispered: "He will make you mad."

Will could neither move nor speak. Something was going on here that was strange indeed.

"I am sorry," she continued. "I did not want to wreck these ships, to drown all within. But I promised."

Will's chill returned. She had drowned them *all*?

He had suspected, but he had not *known*. He had not wanted to.

"What have you done?" he murmured.

The woman, if she was a woman, spun, sparks trailing in the wake of her blindingly white hair. Her eyes were so blue they blazed like twin stars that had fallen from the sky. She flitted toward Will so fast, she appeared there, then here, between one blink and the next. She tilted her head, peering into his face, and afraid—nay, terrified—he snatched her shoulders and shook her.

"What have you done?" he repeated.

She gasped, and instantly he released her. Will was strong, and while he must know the truth, he did not want her hurt.

"You see me?" she asked.

"Of course."

Was she a ghost? No ghost he'd ever met glowed. Besides, all the spirits Will had spoken to had come to *him*, knowing what he was, that he could see and hear them, which was why they *had* come.

"I am invisible," she said.

"Not to me."

The lovely woman extended her hands, frowning at them. "No human should see me. Hear, yes. See, never, unless I will it."

Therein lay the explanation. Will hadn't been human in centuries.

She lifted her gaze, her frown deepening. "How came you here and breathing?"

Her eyes lowered to his chest, and Will made certain to draw in and out, slow and steady, like a goodly fake human.

He did not know what she was, what powers she possessed. Until he did, it would be best that she not know what powers he had.

"I floated upon the waves," he lied. "They brought me here. With them." He indicated the dead sprinkled grotesquely across the beach.

"'Tis impossible," she muttered. "'Tis—"

"Ariel!" They both started as the booming male voice filled the sky. "Come to me, sprite, and be quick."

Her lips pressed together. "All hail, great master," she muttered. "Grave sir, hail! I come."

If her great master heard the sarcasm in her tone, Will thought he would not be pleased.

"Hold." Will touched her arm. "All are dead, you say?"

She nodded, her long, shining hair tumbling over her breasts. Though they were extremely nice breasts, Will barely spared them a glance. He was interested in only one set, and he feared he would never see them again.

"I was ordered to bring the tempest," she whispered, "and I dared not disobey."

"Who is it that calls you, who orders you to toss the seas and murder unsuspecting travelers?"

She shook her head. He tightened his grip on her arm, but the next instant she was gone, and he was left holding nothing but dew.

Sprite, the voice had called her, and Ariel, which must be her name. A sprite was another word for spirit, but Will did not think her a ghost. She controlled the weather, hinted of spells. Mayhap a fairy. Or—

"Elf," he murmured. In very olde England, they'd been called *ylfe,* mischievous beings and exquisitely beautiful, as professed by the word *aelfsciene,* or elf-beautiful. He had never seen one, but he had heard they could be both helpful and harmful.

In truth, did it really matter *what* she was? What mattered was *that* she was and what she had done.

Killed everyone upon both the *Anna Gale* and Will's own ship, ending any hope he might have of a happy un-life.

Will lifted his face to the waning moon and wished for an instant that it were the sun. But no matter.

The sun *would* rise, and then, instead of moving deeper into the jungle and burrowing beneath thick foliage like the nocturnal animal he was, he would stay right here and greet the dawn.

"Truly not the morning sun of heaven," he whispered.

Because it would send him straight to hell.

Chapter Seven

"You play me false."

—*The Tempest* (Act V, scene 1)

Ariel arrived upon the distant beach to discover her master in
a frenzy, pacing back and forth, muttering, and throwing up
his hands.

She dropped from the sky into his path, kneeling and bow-
ing her head. When he was like this, it was best to play humble
or risk being returned to her confinement in the dreaded pine
from whence he had released her.

Ariel was of the fey. A magical spirit, she had fallen to the
earth when it was new. She had spent years, decades, mayhap
centuries, wandering, searching for a place that felt like hers.

The instant she saw this isle, she had been enraptured. Unfortunately, the evil witch Sycorax had already been here, and
she had not been one to share.

When Ariel had refused to do her bidding, Sycorax cast a
spell and confined her within a tree. But a witch was not a fairy.
Sycorax had eventually died. However, the spell did not die
with her.

Ariel had feared she would be forever held within the cloven pine's trunk—a fate much worse than death—confined with no hope of ever seeing the sun, feeling the wind, walking again upon her blessed isle—then Prospero had arrived with his own brand of magic. He had released her, but she was bound to do his will until he agreed that she was not.

"I have come to answer thy best pleasure," she said, "be't to fly, to swim, to dive into the fire, to ride on curl'd clouds, to thy strong bidding task."

"Tricksy spirit," Prospero murmured. "Where hast thou been?"

Ariel lifted her head. His wrath still hovered very near the surface; she must tread lightly.

Did he know what she had done? Or perhaps he had discovered what she had not?

"Sir, thy service have I performed since I went. Upon the far beach more dead await thy pleasure."

His gaze narrowed. "You have killed all upon the ships?"

"You ordered all men to die, and die they have."

Except for that one. She did not know why.

"Explain him." Prospero lifted his chin.

Ariel spun, fearing the dark, handsome, sad-eyed fellow from the far beach had somehow followed her here. Instead, a monster loomed from the trees.

Though her heart took a leap, she did not flee. She was a fairy, a sprite; whatever this was could not hurt her.

The body of a well-made man was covered in sandy fur. His hands, head, and feet appeared those of a wolf, with long sharp claws and teeth. He walked on two legs and not four, his gait swaying and as unnatural as he was.

"I do not understand," she said.

"You do not understand?" A human voice emerged from the wolf's snout, and blue, human eyes glittered madly. "He"—a paw jabbed in Prospero's direction—"has ruined me!"

"From whence did he come, master?"

Prospero threw out his arm toward the sea, and Ariel contemplated the steady, rolling waves. That he had come from the tempest, and that he could see her when she had not allowed it, proved one thing.

"He is not a man," she blurted. This was not her fault.

"I am!" the creature shouted. "I am a baron; I am wealthy. I am Reginald Dymond, and I demand to be put back the way I was."

Then again perhaps the fault *was* hers. She had cast a spell to save the diamond. She had not realized there were two.

Ariel glanced at Prospero, spread her hands, and shrugged. "My spell was quite specific," she said. That much was true. "And do you not remember? You ordered me invisible to all sight but thine and mine."

Prospero's eyes narrowed. "He sees thee."

"Aye," Ariel agreed. "If he were a man, he would not be breathing upon this isle."

Which might explain the presence of the other. Either he was not human, or mayhap he, too, was a diamond. How many could there be?

"That was what I thought," Prospero said. "He is not a man but a beast, and so I cast him as a caliban—the monstrousness upon the inside, now visible to all upon the outside."

Ariel lifted one brow. The stranger did not seem so horrible. She returned her gaze to her master. She had met far worse.

Prospero kept Ariel in bondage so he could make use of her

power over the storm. Within that book he carried everywhere lay a spell that raised the dead—back not to life but to a
strange, shambling un-life.

However, the zombies followed their maker; they would
do anything he asked. Prospero had plans, but to see them to
fruition he needed an army. A zombie army. The only way
to get one on a deserted island was to wreck ship after ship
after ship, watch the bodies roll in, and then raise them.

Ariel returned her gaze to the furry creature. She was not
sure who he was—right now she did not know *what* he was—
but that was for later. When she could converse with him
alone. At the moment there were more pressing issues at hand.

"Sire, your dead await."

"Good counsel, my spirit! The sun will soon be up. I'd best
raise them and move them beneath the trees. The heat does
them little good."

Prospero strode off without so much as a good-bye.

"He is mad," Reginald murmured.

Sometimes Ariel did wonder.

"He told me once a demi-devil, the servant of a bastard,
marooned him on this island."

"Mad indeed," Reginald said. "Mayhap that is why he was
left here."

"Mayhap," Ariel agreed.

Though according to her master, he had been sent away because he was a secret heir to a throne across the sea. A throne
he would reclaim with the aid of his coming zombie army.

"Have you a sword?" she asked.

"'Twas lost in the ocean." Reginald held out his paws before
him. "Not that I would be able to wield it with these. But . . ."

He lowered his arms. "I should probably not kill him until he puts me back the way I was."

"Kill whom?"

"The old man. Why else would I have need of my sword?"

"To fight the zombies."

"Zombies?" His eyes widened, and he began to laugh. "You are as mad as he."

Chapter Eight

"I would not wish any companion in the world but you."

—*The Tempest* (Act III, scene 1)

I snatched up the sword as the *tibonage* emerged from the trees. There were too many. I would never survive.

"Help me," I shouted, hoping the sprite was still there. Ariel had magic; she had brought the storm. Could she not do something about the zombies?

As I received no response to my plea, nor any visible help, I assumed Ariel could do nothing, or that she had already fled.

"Brrr!" the zombies announced as one, their dead eyes fixed on me. All were newly made. None had yet begun to rot.

They would. They could not help it.

However, the more fresh brains the *tibonage* consumed, the slower the rotting commenced. If what Ariel had said was true, and all hands on board had died, I was the sole source of sustenance left on this isle. They were after my brain, but I did not intend to let them have it. I tightened my fingers around the hilt of the sword as they advanced.

At least not without a fight.

I brought up the weapon, slicing off the head of the first

corpse that shambled close. Ashes rained down, then swiftly blew away upon the sultry breeze. I had Ariel to thank for tearing off my sodden, heavy gown, though not for much else. If I ever saw her again—or at all—I might be tempted to lop off *her* head as well.

My Nounou had always advised: *Never fight more than four of the* tibonage *at one time.*

I had broken that rule on occasion, but never like this. There were at least a dozen. However, I had not chosen the battle; the battle had chosen me. I could give up and die, or I could fight.

Luckily the *tibonage* are stupid. If they'd all rushed me at once, the skirmish would have been over and my brains theirs. But while they were able to chant "brrr" in tandem, at first only one fiend at a time tottered in my direction. I dispatched them with ridiculous ease.

However, as their need for sustenance increased, so would their desperation. Driven by hunger, they would surge forward, and I would be overrun.

Though I hated the thought of fleeing, I hated the thought of dying even more, so I sidestepped with every swipe, inching closer and closer to the trees. When their shadow fell upon me, I dashed away.

"Brrr!" shouted the *tibonage,* voices lifting in surprised unison.

I had no shoes. Small stones and sticks jabbed my feet. Branches tugged at my hair and slapped my face and arms. Shrubbery sliced my legs. Better that than teeth tearing into my head.

Zombies shamble; they do not run, but there are times, especially when they are new and nothing has yet fallen off, that they shamble very quickly indeed.

I glanced back and nearly fell on my face to discover the fiends far too close behind.

I was accustomed to the click of their toenails on stones. Most *tibonage* are raised from graves and not right away. Though the body may die, the hair, the nails, continue to grow, creating a familiar *snick* against the road or sometimes the kitchen floor. I had saved myself many a time by swinging my sword in an arc toward that telltale *snick* as it approached from behind. Without it I felt almost bereft.

I increased my speed, ducked behind a tree, then ran to the next and darted right before going straight ahead for two tree lengths then taking another quick right. When I glanced back again, I was alone.

"God's belt loops," I muttered. That had been close.

Too on edge to remain still, I continued on, my mind at work on the problem. According to the sprite, this was Zombie Island. I knew not why. I knew not how. But I would find out.

If I lived long enough.

I wished once more for Will's comforting presence. He was not only strong and fast and extremely hard to kill, but he was so very, very smart. I could use his clever brain, along with his solid sword arm.

We had been apart only days, but my heart yearned as if we had been apart a lifetime. Probably because we would be apart for a lifetime. Or at least my lifetime.

Even if I managed, somehow, to slay all the zombies, what then? I could not swim back to England, and Will had no idea where I'd gone. No one did. My chances of rescue were slimmer than the tip of my sword.

However, that was a problem for another day. Today I

needed a place to hide. Later I could sneak out and end the *ti-bonage* one by one.

Having a plan lightened a heart gone heavy with the loss of Will. I had led a lonely life—an only child, my mother dead in childbirth, my father not an affectionate man. I'd had high hopes for my marriage, which were dashed soon after the wedding. The loss of Nounou had increased my isolation. I'd thrown myself into my calling, venting all my neglected desires into becoming the best zombie hunter in the land.

I'd told myself I needed no one, that love was not real. Then I'd found Will and discovered differently. Now I wasn't sure I would survive without him, without love.

My momentary lightness disappeared; the breath I took hitched in the middle like a lost, sobbing child's. If I were trapped here, with nothing but zombies and a strange sprite for company, I might go mad. Perhaps it would be better to end it than to live on like this.

I contemplated the pointy end of my sword. Could I? Most certainly, but—

"Not yet." I dropped the weapon back to my side.

The crash of waves nearby drew my gaze, and I caught sight of another beach through the gaps between the trees. A beach and—

More bodies.

Moving closer, I slid carefully through the foliage so as to create no more sound than a whisper on the wind. I kept to the cool shadows as the sun lightened the horizon. Soon it would burst past the rim of the ocean and spread its blazing light across this land. I would welcome it. Everything always looked brighter in the sun.

A movement caught my eye. A figure stood to my right, just

beyond the edge of the trees, face tilted to greet the inevitable dawn.

Strange. If I didn't know better—

I blinked several times rapidly, squeezed my eyes shut, then let them fly open.

He was still there. His beautiful face, his short-cropped beard, his tangled, curly dark hair, the tiny hoop he wore in one ear, which caught the coming light of the sun, and—

My chest seized. The sun!

I burst from the trees and into the waning starlight. Tossing my sword to the side, I leaped just as he turned—it *was* he!— eyes widening an instant before I crashed into him.

We slammed to the ground, safely out of reach of the sun. My breath left my lungs in a *whoosh*. Then I was kissing him; he was kissing me. The both of us running our hands over each other, my fingers tangling in his hair, his wrapping into mine, as if to prove that we were real and that we would not suddenly disappear.

His mouth so soft, his mustache tickled my lip an instant before his tongue did. I moaned and met that tongue eagerly with my own. I would have been completely carried away, besotted, as I always was when he touched me, if the chill of his skin hadn't reminded me that he could not, should not, stay here.

I tore away, pressing my palm to his forehead and pushing him back down when he would have craned his neck and rained kisses across mine. Though I wanted nothing more than to let him, now was not the time.

"What were you doing?"

At his confused expression—considering the hardness pressing into my belly, I understood his behavior; he might no longer be a breathing man, but still he was a man, and asking him questions in a situation like this usually produced gibberish instead of answers—I continued: "The *sun,* Will!"

His fine, sweet brow furrowed. " 'Tis not yet up."

"Praise the saints," I muttered. "If it had been, you would be dead. Truly dead, forevermore."

"Aye." Sense trickled into his eyes. "I planned to greet it for the first time in centuries."

For an instant regret flashed in his gaze as well, and I kissed that brow. I knew how much he missed the dawn. But—

"Why, Will?" I murmured.

"Without you on this earth, sweet Kate, my life—such that it is—is not worth continuing."

Since I had harbored much the same thoughts not long past, I could not fault him. But I shivered, nevertheless, at the realization of what would have happened if I'd turned in another direction when running from the zombies.

Will would be ashes, and I would be alone.

I kissed him again; I wanted never, ever to stop.

Which was why it took me so long to hear the voice on the beach, followed by a distinct, rumbling, "Brrr!"

I leaped to my feet, narrowly missing Will's privates with my knee. I had retrieved my discarded sword before Will's indrawn hiss faded on the suddenly still air.

Crouched, weapon at the ready, I faced the jungle, expecting the *tibonage* I'd left behind to emerge. But nothing did.

"Kate," Will murmured, lifting his chin to indicate the ocean.

I spun, eyes widening as every dead man on the beach rose.

I'd never seen the dead rise. I'd seen them walk; I'd seen them almost talk. I'd seen them fight and kill and consume.

But I'd never been present when they went from dead to living dead.

I glanced at Will. "Did you . . . ?"

His mouth twisted. "No!"

The only being I knew that could raise zombies was a necro-vampire. A necromancer in life, in undeath his, or her, affinity with the dead could call them from the grave. Will possessed this talent—he had once raised zombie armies for money—but he hadn't used it in years.

I'd known one other necro-vampire. But Will had torn off his head.

I frowned at the crowd of corpses milling about not far enough away. "If not you, then who?"

"It cannot be a necro-vampire," Will murmured.

"Why?"

Will kept his gaze on the walking dead. "As far as I know, the only time we can raise zombies is beneath a full moon. Also . . ." He shifted his shoulders, almost a shrug, but not quite. "I feel others like me. Right now, all I feel is . . ." He grimaced at the creatures. "Bluck."

Bluck?

"Then how . . . ?"

Will shook his head. "No time."

I glanced at the beach. Dozens of eyes gazed back.

"Brrrr!" The *tibonage* shuffled our way, legs stiff, arms outstretched.

"Run, Kate." We turned.

Hell. The creatures I'd escaped earlier now barred our way.

"How many are there?" Will muttered.

"More than there should be."

"One is more than there should be."

The zombies purred their lust for "brr," causing the very air around us to buzz. Prickles of panic danced across my skin. Was this the end for us both?

Then Will swept me into his arms and darted into the jungle. The world became a blur. Everything would have been all right if it hadn't been for the sun.

The foliage was so thick, only a thin band of light came through here and there, dotting the ground before us like sprinkles of golden dew. I wasn't thinking—dazzled by being saved, breathless at our speed, thrilled to again be in Will Shakespeare's arms.

One instant Will was running faster than any human could, the next he was falling; I was flying through the air. We landed at about the same time—him on his face, me on my arse.

"God's spleen," I snapped, rubbing what would no doubt be a sizable bruise.

Will lay as though dead—not a breath stirred his lips, not a beat stirred his heart, not that this would be any different were he awake. However, he would not move until the sun traveled past midday. If we were to escape, I would have to move him.

"Brr!"

And I would have to move him soon.

But he was "dead" weight, and while I was a *chasseur* and strong, I was still a woman. I tugged. I pulled. I shoved. Yet Will barely budged.

I could not leave him. I would not. So I picked up my sword and prepared to protect him. Or die trying.

The thrash and thud of too many feet thundered closer. My palms became wet. Sweat dripped off the end of my nose.

"Fool!"

I glanced up as the high, furious voice poured from the air, yet I saw nothing beyond a slight ripple within a ray of sunlight.

"There are too many. Why stand you there?"

I tightened my fingers around the hilt. "I will not desert him."

"Him?" The ripple hovered over Will. "At last he is dead, as he should be."

"He is not . . ." I paused. Will was *undead*. Which meant he existed, but he did not live. I wasn't sure how to explain that, or if I even should.

"He will rise soon," Ariel continued. "Can you chop off his head now? Will that destroy him, or must you wait until he walks?"

"He will not become a zombie."

"He does not breathe. His skin is cold. No heart beats within his breast."

My gaze narrowed. "Do not touch him."

No one touched Will Shakespeare as he lay sleeping but me.

"Who is he?" Ariel asked.

"My love, my life, my everything." I clutched tight my sword, prepared to face the ravenous, brain-eating horde. "If he dies, then I die too."

The "brrrs" became louder; the *tibonage* crunched upon every stick, kicked every stone, and slashed through the foliage with all the grace of mad cows. Zombies would never be considered light upon their feet.

The first came out of the trees, caught sight of me, of Will, and grinned. His mouth already canted sideways upon his face. The sultry air would rot the creatures faster than any I'd encountered before. Perhaps I could outlast them.

Eight more joined the first. A dozen crowded at their backs.

Or not.

The first charged across the clearing, shouting, "Brrr!" like a battle cry.

The others answered, "Brrrrr!" and followed.

I stepped forward, planting my foot, then swinging my sword with all my might.

The blade sliced through the low-hanging branches of a tree that had not been there an instant before. My momentum carried me around. I nearly sliced off my own ear before I lost my balance and tumbled to the ground.

I waited for them to fall on me, to fall on Will.

Nothing happened.

Lifting my head, I stared in amazement at the thick, soft emerald grass that cushioned our bodies, the canopy of leafy trees that shaded us from the sun, and the waterfall that tumbled into a clear, blue pool at its base.

Chapter Nine

"Good wombs have borne bad sons."
—*The Tempest* (Act I, scene 2)

Ariel would have followed her diamond and the strange should-be-dead-but-was-not man the woman would die for—such behavior was confusing to her, and she wanted to discover its cause—but at that instant, her master called.

"Now come, my Ariel! Appear and pertly!"

Ariel twirled upward, away from the absurdly milling zombies. Their brains were gruel; they did not comprehend why there had been the scent of fresh "brr" then suddenly there was not. So they walked in circles, searching, moaning.

To be fair, those without gruel for brains would be equally confused; however, they might move on more quickly. She suspected the zombies would continue to wear a path in the dirt until they rotted through.

She sped into the dawn, enjoying the spray of the newly born sun upon her face. Though much of her time here of late had been a horror, she adored this island. For the island she would do anything.

Ariel found Prospero on the now empty beach, staring at the equally empty sea.

"Sire," she began.

He spun with lifted finger. "No tongue! All eyes! Be silent."

Ariel pressed her lips together and drifted downward until her bare feet met the deliciously warm sand.

"I have forgotten something."

Your humanity, perchance?

Ariel's lips tightened further. She dared not let *that* escape.

The man sickened her. She might be a sprite, not human herself, but she knew what was wrong and what was right. And this . . .

Ariel's gaze narrowed on Prospero.

This was so wrong.

But she did not know what to do. She had promised her allegiance if he would but set her free, and once promised that bond could not be broken. Until Prospero released her—*if* he released her—Ariel was his slave.

"The zombies need nourishment." Prospero tapped his cursed magic book. "If they do not have fresh brains, they will rot. How can I build an army if the hands of the first risen soldiers fall off before I can lift enough of them to be of any use?"

He frowned, the expression causing the lines in his face to deepen and his blue eyes to darken like the sea on a moonless night. "'Twill be a problem," he murmured. "I thought I could build my army ship by ship, storm by storm. But if they must be fed . . ." His lips tightened; he rubbed his head. "If only I could raise the entire army in one swoop. But I do not have the strength for that much magic."

The weight that had lived on Ariel's breast since this had

begun lightened. "Ah well," she said. "You tried. 'Tis done." No more storms, no more death, no more—

"Done?" he shouted. "Bite thy tongue! Let it fall from thy mouth and onto the sand! Never speak such again!"

Ariel lifted her hands to her lips, afraid his words were a spell that would indeed cause her to bite off her own tongue. But she yet had control of herself.

"All we must do," he continued more quietly, "is feed them."

The weight returned to Ariel's chest. She wondered if she would ever get it off.

"This need for brains." Ariel inched closer, trying to see into the book, but Prospero snapped it shut. "Should you not have known this before? It seems an important detail."

Her master shrugged, and Ariel understood. The man had once again neglected to read the instructions.

This had happened before, with similar disastrous results. Prospero had attempted to perform a transportation spell and hie himself back to England. He'd wound up far out in the sea, and only Ariel's intervention had saved his life.

But had he, in his gratitude, released her? Of course not. He was as single-minded in his devotion to his nefarious plan as the zombies he raised for it would be. Ariel should have let the fool drown, but she was powerless to ignore his commands.

Ariel could have told him if he'd but asked that transportation only worked over a short distance. For instance, she could move about this island, as could he.

If he but read the damn instructions.

Then there was the time Prospero had decided he had a taste for mutton. He'd attempted to change a seabird into a sheep. Ariel stifled a wince at the horrific thing he had produced. It had flown away bleating.

She didn't even want to think about the creature he'd created when he'd tried to transform a fish into a woman. As he had told her, "Men have needs." But no one needed *that*. Out there in the ocean somewhere was a woman with gills, a tail, and great big—

"Ariel?" Prospero snapped his fingers in front of her nose. "The point is not that I misjudged, the point is that we need fresh brains."

Ariel thought that not the point at all, but she would not argue.

"What is within your head will not be enough to feed the lot," she murmured.

"Not mine, fine spirit." He pointed toward the sea. "Theirs."

Ariel turned. Several brilliant white sails fluttered against the crystal blue sky. Ariel swallowed her rising horror. "But, sire, more dead will only mean more starving, rotting fiends."

"Not dead, Ariel, not this time." Prospero smiled, and the expression was that of a cat who had uncovered the nest of a mouse. "Create a lull. Strand them near, have the waves pull them in."

Despite the warm breeze, the heated sun, and the lack of anything resembling blood in Ariel's glimmering body, she shivered. A waterfall of sparks fell to the ground and bounced around her feet like droplets of water atop a steaming griddle.

"And then?" she whispered.

"They will come ashore. How can they help themselves? Our isle is beauty itself. Once safely on land"—his lips still held that murderous cat-smile—"you will move the ships to a safe harbor, in the deep nook, where once I call'dst you up at midnight to fetch dew. They will be here; their ships will be . . ." He waved his arm. "There, and voilà! Nourishment."

Nourishment? Ariel thought.

More like a bloodbath.

"Spirit, you seem upset. Have you trouble with my plan?" He lifted a bushy red-and-white brow then opened his book, licked one finger, and began to page through. "Where is that lovely spell to put you back in the tree?"

Since *that* spell he would no doubt get just right, Ariel lifted her arms.

And the wind did still.

Chapter Ten

"The air breathes upon us here most sweetly."
—*The Tempest* (Act II, scene 1)

I stood guard over Will. Though the glade seemed enchanted, a place far away and safe from the rest of the isle, every so often, in the distance, I heard a shriek. Mayhap it was a bird or a wild cat; who knew what other dangers lurked about.

But Ariel had brought me here to slay zombies; she had called the place Zombie Island; I had seen for myself the herd of *tibonage* that roamed; and I had done this work for long enough to have a sense of it.

We were safe for now, but it would not do to forget that in truth no one was safe anywhere at all.

Whilst I waited for the sun to climb high enough that Will would wake, I broke my fast with the luscious fruits that fell at my feet from some of the mysterious trees. I used my sword—cleaned well in the pool—to crack open the hard, deep-green-and-red shell of one to discover an inside of bright orange that tasted like ambrosia and spouted forth enough juice to quench my thirst as well as stanch my hunger.

When I had finished making a glutton of myself, I knelt by

the pool to wash the sticky remnants from my hands and face. The water was so clear, the temperature so perfect, I was tempted to slide in completely, wash the salt from my hair and shift, scrub the zombie ash from my neck. But I would not leave Will unprotected.

Then, as if his spirit had heard my thoughts, his image was reflected at my back. I would have thought him a ghost, except when the figure reached for my shoulder, an actual hand landed upon it.

"Kate," he murmured, and I laced my fingers with his.

His skin was cool, though not unpleasant; I'd always found it refreshing. His image dropped as he went to his knees. Then his arms came about me, and his chin rested atop my head. "I thought I'd lost you."

My eyes stung at the stark fear in his voice. "You didn't."

I leaned against his chest. His forest green doublet, stiffened by seawater, scratched my shoulders. I wanted him to take it off, to take everything off, but not yet. First he needed, *we* needed, to talk.

"When I went to the crypt, and you weren't there, I—" His voice broke, and he paused, throat working.

I could imagine, *had* imagined. Poor man.

"How did you find me?" I trailed my fingers over his hand. He had such beautiful hands. Long, slim fingers that could wield both a quill and a sword with equal fervor, yet stroke a woman into a fever.

Dear Lord, I loved those hands.

"Nounou," he said.

"Ah." I should have known. The ghost of my old nurse spoke often to Will. Her wise counsel was proving to be as beneficial now as it had been when she was alive.

"Is she here?" I asked. 'Twould be a comfort.

The lips reflected upon the water turned downward. "I have not seen her since I left the crypt. Mayhap she cannot leave England."

"I am unfamiliar with the rules that govern ghosts," I said.

"As am I," he murmured. "Although I have seen Italian spirits in your bedchamber in London."

I stiffened so fast my head nearly caught him in the chin. "What?" I had the sudden image of ghosts lining my bedchamber, watching me undress, watching Will and me—

"When?" I demanded.

"Shh." He ran his palm over my hair and, immediately, my tension flowed away. He had that effect on me. When Will was near, the rest of the world seemed so far. "Remember the two gentlemen?"

"Of Verona? Aye." The new play he had written. Its opening night had been marred by a near zombie apocalypse, a plot to kill the queen, foiled by us. "Valentine and Proteus."

"How do you think I learned their story?"

"I thought it sprang from your head. Isn't that where all good ideas begin?"

He stroked me again, and though his hand remained cool—when was it not?—I began to feel quite warm. "The words are mine. The plays are often tales told to me by my ghosts."

"*Your* ghosts?" I caught his wince and tightened my fingers on his. I knew he saw ghosts, that they spoke to him. But beyond that, I had not had time to learn more. "Will, you can tell me anything. There is nothing you can say that will make me not love you."

He gave a delicate snort. "Kate, you are so very, very young."

"Compared to you a crone is young," I muttered, and he

laughed. I refused to be distracted from my course. "Why are they 'your' ghosts?"

His laughter died as quickly as it had been born. "Many of the ghosts who speak to me do so because I made them that way."

Suddenly I understood. The creature that had turned Will into a vampire had left him alone to discover on his own what that meant. He had given Will no instruction, no knowledge of how to fight the bloodlust within. Most likely because the horrible man—nay, the horrible *thing*—had never bothered to fight his own urge to kill but had rather embraced it.

According to Will, once the initial frenzy had passed, vampires become again who they were. As Will had been a gentle, poetic soul before he'd become undead, he was now again. Which meant that fiendish vampires had been fiendish humans at one time. The more humans I met, the more I understood how this could easily occur.

"You tell upon the stage the stories of those who have died by your . . ." I paused, thought, then settled on, "Hand."

Will rolled his eyes. "It is the least I can do."

"The Henrys?" I asked. I did not think the death by vampire of several English kings could have been brushed over by history.

"Some wanted zombie armies."

"Ah."

"I did not know." His sigh revealed all he did not say.

When the creature had changed Will from man to vampire, he had not known Will was a necromancer. Mayhap he had not even known what that would mean.

"I was confused," he continued. "I did not understand what living forever would mean. The cost—" He broke off.

I was not sure if he meant the cost in human life or in actual pounds. Will must have seen the question reflected upon my face, as he answered without my ever having to ask.

"I raised those armies for money."

"You do not do so any longer," I soothed.

"Nay." He shuddered, though his blood was too cold for him to ever *be* cold.

"And why do you write those stories?" It would not seem that he owed a tyrant king anything.

"They haunt me," he said simply, "and forever is a very long time."

Another clue tumbled into place. "You write of what you know."

"What I have seen and heard, those I have met," he agreed.

"There are people who say you steal your ideas from other sources."

In the still water, his lips curved. "Who is to say those other sources were not me in the first place?"

A single thread of laughter escaped me. "Who indeed?"

His arms again tightened round me, and for several moments we knelt in each other's arms. This idyll would not last, and we knew it.

"I was so frightened, Kate."

I disentangled myself from his embrace and sat at the edge of the water. He joined me, and I took his hand. "Nounou told you what had happened?"

"Aye."

"How came you here?"

He was a vampire, but he was not a magician. His appearance on this isle was most strange.

"I commandeered the next ship."

When Will said "commandeered," I understood exactly what he meant. He had pushed. A handy talent, and one he had used on me.

Once. He knew better than to ever do so again.

"The captain saw this place," Will said. "It disturbed him."

"How so?"

"It was not on any of his charts. He had never seen it before."

"There *is* something odd about it."

"Mayhap the elf," Will muttered.

"There is an elf too?"

"Too?" Will's eyes, which had widened with surprise, now narrowed. "What have you seen?"

"Nothing. I merely heard a voice. She said she was a sprite."

"Ariel."

I straightened. "You heard her as well?"

"Heard *and* saw. A beautiful, silver woman, with white hair and sparkling blue eyes."

"A silver woman," I repeated. Will shrugged. "Wore she clothes like mine?" I indicated my skirt then realized it was gone. "Mine before she tore them free."

"She wore no clothes at all."

I blinked. "And you did not think to mention this?"

"To tell you true, Kate, I barely noticed."

I gave a delicate snort. "No man would fail to notice a naked woman. Be she silver or no."

"I am not a man."

"You brandish a rod like one," I muttered. In truth, he brandished it better than most.

He squeezed my hand until I lifted my gaze to his. "I love you more than words can wield the matter, dearer than eyesight, space, and liberty."

"Lovely," I breathed. "You must write that down."

His precious lips lifted. "Another sonnet to my Dark Lady?"

"Better than an ode to your silvery one."

"There is no woman in the world for me but you."

"Nor man for me but you," I returned.

We sealed this with a kiss, and when we were through, Will glanced around the enchanted glade. "How came we here? The last I remember I was carrying you away from far too many zombies."

"The sun came up."

Will winced. "I left you to fight them alone."

My behind still ached from the thumping it had taken when he dropped me, but I managed not to rub the sore spot. He felt bad enough. "You did not leave," I pointed out. "And I did not have to fight. Ariel spirited us away. One minute there, the next here."

"She truly is magic."

"She commands the wind and the water," I said. "Which allows her to bring the storms."

"Which killed all aboard the ships."

"Do you think she raised the zombies?"

"Perhaps." Will frowned. "Though she said she had—"

"Promised," we repeated as one.

"Someone controls her," Will murmured.

My gaze met his. "How many beings are on this island?"

Chapter Eleven

"O brave new world, that has such people in't!"

—*The Tempest* (Act V, scene 1)

Reginald Dymond loped down an overgrown path. After several disastrous attempts to run on two legs, he'd discovered he could move much faster and more easily on four paws.

The fur that covered his body protected him from the slash of branches. The thick pads upon what had once been his feet and hands kept any stray stones from cutting him.

His nose, not much larger now than when he'd been completely human, nevertheless worked so much better. In times past, he'd sniffled and sneezed whenever he'd come close to flowers and trees. But presently his nostrils were clear, and he relished the symphony of scents all around.

His eyes, too, were a marvel. He no longer needed to squint. He could see near; he could see far. The colors were as glorious as the smells. It had been so long since he'd been able to see individual leaves—for years all trees had merely appeared like one great circle of green on a stick—he paused often to sit on his haunches and stare.

On four paws he was graceful. He could run without tripping;

he could leap and land without falling. He was fast. He was strong.

He was amazing.

After the beautiful silver woman had disappeared—literally—from the beach, Reginald had concluded he was either dead or dreaming.

A silver woman who spoke of zombies?

An old man who called himself lord of a temperate isle where there could *be* no such place?

The island itself—beautiful beyond imagining.

And Reginald—become half man, half beast.

Things like that did not happen. Places like this did not exist. Creatures like Ariel did not walk upon the earth.

Therefore, he was dead and in heaven, or dreaming and back on the ship. Since Reginald was enjoying himself—and he had found precious little to enjoy of late—he would continue to do just that.

His clothes had torn away. He did not mind. They had been heavy, hot, and they'd made his new body itch. With his nakedness covered by fine, blond fur, he did not feel exposed but rather—

"Freed." The word came out a low-voiced, intimidating growl, and he laughed, delighted. Even when his laughter sounded very like the bark of a dog, he did not care.

So much running had made him thirsty, so he lifted his once unfortunate but now incredible nose to the air and caught the scent of fresh water. How utterly convenient.

Pointing his claws in that direction, he ran. Every so often he would sniff again, either continue on his course or alter it slightly, until, mayhap five sniffs later, he caught a putrid scent that made him stop.

His upper lip curled in revulsion. He reared onto his hind legs as a snarl gurgled in his throat. The hair along his back lifted. Something was not right.

They emerged from the trees like a nightmare. Ah yes, he *was* dreaming, but the dream had turned dark.

"Thou shalt be pinch'd," he muttered, then did so, grasping a tiny bit of his fur-covered flesh with a claw.

The pain made him jump. It did not make the creatures go away. Rather, at the sight of him they advanced, murmuring something that sounded like "Brrr!"

"As thick as honeycomb," he continued. "Each pinch more stinging than bees that made 'em." Reginald pinched himself several more times, with similar results, which, in truth, were no results at all since he continued to dream.

They smelled of the ocean, beneath a seasoning of rot, and their clothes, what were left of them, were much like the clothes of those who worked the *Anna Gale*. In truth, several of the faces resembled men he'd seen upon her decks.

'Twas impossible, of course, but then so much upon this island was.

"What are you?" he asked, retreating as they advanced.

"Brr!" they answered, then commenced a horrible gnashing of teeth.

Several sprouted putrefying sores, which explained the aroma of decay. They dragged their feet; they were quite slow. If not, they would already have fallen upon him.

Oddly, while Reginald was disgusted—that smell, the sight, their sounds—he was not afraid. With his new form he could outrun them. Mayhap he could even—

The foremost man, if man he could yet be called, moved more quickly than Reginald had believed him capable. He swept his arms toward Reginald, as if he would hug him close.

Reginald yanked his overly long nose free of the snapping teeth with very little room to spare. The fellow's spittle sprayed Reginald's snout, and horrified, he howled then swiped out with his right claw.

The creature's head separated from the shoulders. Before it could bounce at Reginald's feet, both that head and the still upright body turned to ashes and collapsed with a soft *whoosh*.

Reginald stared at the pile on the ground. He would have continued to do so until the warm breeze blew all away, but the other creatures—*admit it, Dymond, they are zombies*—advanced.

What worked once worked very well again, and he swiped right, left, right again, aiming for their throats. In very little time at all, he was alone with nothing but ashes. The silence after so much "brrr!" was exquisite.

Reginald stared at his claws. So sharp! How efficient! What need would he ever have again for hands?

He was starting to believe himself both awake and alive. He had come upon a place not of this world; he had become something other than what he'd been. He should be pounding his chest and crying for justice. Instead . . .

A strange emotion filled him. It took Reginald several moments to conclude it was pride. He had never felt such a thing before.

He was an ugly man. Not his fault, yet he had been blamed. Now—

He gently touched his snout with his paw. No bigger than before, no uglier. But much more useful, as were—

"These," he rumbled, holding out his claws and admiring

them. He had dispatched those horrible creatures with ease. They'd deserved nothing less.

And he'd been good at it. Reginald could not remember ever being good at anything in his life.

He had not done well in school. He had been teased; he'd made very few friends. His attention often wandered.

He had done equally poorly with love. The only reason Kate had married him was for his pedigree—he was the distant relation of an earl. He had "good blood." Even the plantation her father had ordered Reginald to manage had turned a profit only because of the overseer his father-in-law had hired. Reginald wasn't a farmer. He knew nothing of tobacco. The place had become a success not because of him but in spite of him.

However, here, like this—he waggled his claws—Reginald Dymond—nay, *Caliban*—was king. It no longer mattered if he resembled a beast. As the old fellow had said, his inside was merely visible now on the outside. Which was good. If he appeared a beast, no one would expect him to be anything else.

His greatest difficulty had always arisen whenever Reginald attempted to be the most human.

Chapter Twelve

"Hear my soul speak: The very instant that
I saw you, did my heart fly to your service."
—*The Tempest* (Act III, scene 1)

Kate rose to her knees as if to stand. Will did the same but set his hands upon her shoulders, staying her. Her confused expression lay reflected in the clear, blue pool along with their images.

"Should we not find out how many others are on this isle?" she asked.

Will leaned forward, placing his lips to his love's ear. "I thought I had lost you. Can we spend a few moments to find each other again?"

Her confusion fled before her smile. "A few moments? Did you miss me that little?"

Pain shot through his chest at the memory. He'd thought he would miss her for eternity.

"Why did your husband take your dead body along on his trip to the New World?"

"I wasn't dead."

"*He* did not know that."

Kate's eyes widened, and she gasped. Will reached for his

sword, which was no longer there. Hers lay a few feet away, but instead of diving for it, she turned in his arms. The joy on her face stilled his panic.

"What is it?" he asked.

"Reginald was on the ship?"

"Aye." Suddenly Will understood. "He is dead. At the bottom of the sea."

"I should have thought of that before, but the zombies, the island, it overwhelmed me."

"This has overwhelmed us both." Will's lips curved. "Sometimes fate is just."

"I shouldn't be happy about this," Kate murmured. "It is not right."

"He treated you badly." The first time Will had met the man, he'd struck Kate across the face in front of the queen. Every time Will thought of it, his teeth itched.

Of course, it wasn't unusual for husbands to strike their wives, and to be fair, Dymond had believed Kate pregnant and not by him. Still—

Will was glad the bastard was dead.

"He did," Kate agreed. "Though not as badly as he might have."

Will was certain what Kate had shared with him about her husband—the man's vocal disgust for her "unfashionable" appearance, his treating of her as a brood mare and little else, his unreasonable jealousy considering he cared about her not a whit, the setting of his old nurse upon her as a spy, and his habit of locking her in a room if she annoyed him—had been only a small part of what she had endured, but he decided to let the comment pass. The man was dead. Nothing would be gained from speaking ill of him.

"We should—" Kate began, and Will took her in his arms.

"Aye," he agreed, putting his lips to her hair. "We should."

The pool at her back reflected their embrace, and the beauty of the image, the deep-down rightness of it, made a heart that no longer beat long to. Just for her.

"Look." Will turned Kate toward the pool. "Look at you, sweet Kate, look at us."

Will fondled a small yet perfect breast, and Kate's eyes slid closed. Thank goodness the nonsense about vampires not casting a reflection was just that. Watching himself touch her, observing the splendor of her face, even as her exquisite rump pressed into his steadily hardening cock, made Will harden all the more. He had come so close to losing her; he desperately wanted to make her his again.

"Us," Kate murmured, arching against him.

The movement rubbed her nipple along the center of his palm. He had to fight the urge to tear his own clothes from his body then remove hers with equal fervor.

She tilted her head, and her hair swung away from the nape, exposing the fine line of her throat. He placed his mouth to the vein that throbbed there, grazing it with his teeth.

"Yes," she whispered, cupping her fingers about his neck, pressing him closer, offering him everything.

She trusted him implicitly, believed he would not drink from her, that even in the heat of their passion he would not forget and do her injury.

Of course, it had been easier before he'd tasted her. Now that he knew the flavor of Kate's blood, would it call to him? Would he be able to resist? This was the first time they had been together like this since he had nearly killed her. Could he trust himself? Should she?

Will lifted his mouth, closed his eyes, counted to ten, and thought of puppies, kittens, sweet, fluffy gamboling spring lambs. His fangs, which had begun to itch at the memory of Kate's blood on his tongue, retracted.

He never should have sipped from her sweet vein. But he'd had little choice. In order to gain the strength necessary to save both Kate and the queen then destroy the necro-vampire that had set zombies upon London, Will had needed blood. At the time, the necks of Kate and Queen Bess were the only ones available.

Not even Kate knew how near he'd been to losing control, how close she'd come to dying in his arms, and he hoped she never would.

Kate saw him as a man with a monstrous affliction. Will knew himself to be a monster that would never again be completely a man.

But, oh, how he wanted to.

"Will?" she murmured, her fingers trailing through his hair. She still posed with her delicate throat exposed, her eyes closed, trusting utterly that he would not hurt her.

He swore he would die rather than do so. Of course, he had sworn the same thing before and—

Will pushed the memory from his mind. Thinking of the past helped only when writing. When living—or whatever it was that Will did—thinking of the past caused only pain.

"Kate," he responded, and slipped his finger beneath the fine, once white chemise. He slid it back and forth over her nipple until the bud had become as hard as he was, then he turned his attentions to the other.

Kate could not realize she was rubbing her back against his front in a delicious movement that made him want to release himself from his breeches, bend her over, and take her while they still wore most of their clothes.

She reached around and tugged on his laces, her nimble, clever fingers opening them then dipping within before he could gather his thoughts and stop her. He nearly humiliated himself right then.

He grasped her hips, stilling her, and their gazes met in the pool. Her hair curled wildly around her face. The darker shade of her skin shone darker still against the white undergarment. He knew she hated the unfashionably sun-ripened hue, but he loved it. He loved everything about her.

"Take me, Will." Her hand, still wrapped around him, tightened. "Now. Here. Like this. I want to watch."

He gulped. How did she know his most intimate thoughts? Mayhap because they were hers as well. He and Kate had forever been like-minded.

Slowly he lifted the shortened skirt of her chemise. Beneath he found nothing but Kate. He ran his palms up the sides of her glorious thighs, slim and hard from nights spent chasing zombies, until he reached firm curves. Then he paused, uncertain.

She was his love, his life. He should not—

Kate fell forward, hands planted on the soft grass, head lifted so she could watch him—watch them—in the pool. Her back arched as she offered herself.

No man could resist. And Will, who was not a man, had less resistance than most. With Kate, he had none.

He buried himself within her. The reflection in the water shimmered—breaking apart, then coming back together, as they did. The sight of Kate on her hands and knees, her breasts swaying with the power of his thrusts, her face revealing the ecstasy within, caused Will to slow, afraid he would finish long before he wanted to.

At the cessation of his movements, Kate glanced back. When their eyes met, all the love he felt for her hit him in the chest, and if he'd been breathing, he thought he would have stopped.

"Kate," was all he managed before she performed an agile twist so that she lay upon the ground in front of him, arms open—an invitation, a promise. He sank into her again, face-to-face.

She lifted her mouth; he took the offering, kissing her, tasting her, basking in the memories of before, even as he memorized forever the now.

She tasted of grapes birthed in the sun. Her embrace spread through him like warm Madeira, and even though she'd been dunked in brine, he could still catch the faint scent of roses in her hair.

"You have witchcraft in your lips," he murmured against them.

"'Tis just love," she returned. "She will die if you love her not."

As often happened when he was with her, when he was within her, Will's muse awoke. Most likely because Kate *was* his muse, and when they became one all he saw, all he heard and felt and knew, was her.

His fingertips brushed her cheek, and the words in his mind, in his heart, spilled free. "Doubt thou the stars are fire. Doubt that the sun doth move. Doubt truth to be a liar. But never doubt I love."

Her smile was the morning sun for which he pined. "Never," she agreed.

"Forever," he returned.

Or at least for as long as she lived.

Something must have flickered in Will's eyes—despair, pain, horror—for Kate frowned and touched his face. "Will?"

A strange whisper came from the trees, as if the earth had heard his thoughts and exhaled a sigh that held the sadness of the ages.

His gaze sought the sound, but Kate's voice—"Is aught amiss?"—brought him sharply back. Something was, but he would not speak of it.

"Hush," he murmured, then made certain that she did. He would not mar their reunion, their love, their joy, with thoughts of separation and death. Just because he was inclined toward darkness of mind and soul did not mean she should have to be.

Her gasp of completion fueled his own, made him forget—at least for the moment—the shortness of human life, the frailty of the human condition.

When it was over, and he lay in her arms, when she lay in his, Will stared at the canopy of trees, listening to the birds, the water, Kate's breath.

He would love her all of her life.

Then he would mourn her for the eternity that was his.

Chapter Thirteen

"Sometime am I all wound with adders who with
cloven tongues do hiss me into madness."

—*The Tempest* (Act II, scene 2)

Reginald had spent the morning trolling the trees for zombies. He didn't have to go far. The bastards were everywhere.

They rotted quickly in the heat. With every new one he found, the stench of them increased. Soon he was no longer looking for them at all but merely following his wondrous nose.

His fur gray with ashes, he panted as he ran, his overly long tongue lolling out of his mouth. When he caught the scent of fresh water in the distance, a yip of pleasure escaped him.

But the jungle thickened. If he had not been able to move on four paws, lower to the ground, pulling himself along with his claws, making use of new and amazing strength he had never before had, Reginald would not have reached the pool. As it was, he wished he hadn't.

His eyes! He thought they might catch fire in his head from the devilish scene that he witnessed.

The man and the woman were—

Reginald glanced away and huffed air through his nose then pawed at the appendage when it tickled. He barely missed poking out an eye with a claw, and perhaps that would have been best, because when he returned his gaze to the tableau in front of him, he found himself no longer able to glance away.

The man and the woman were fornicating. Right out in the open. He hadn't even removed his clothes, or all of hers, though he'd at least stripped her to her chemise.

However, it wasn't the act that held Reginald's attention—although he'd never watched before and discovered the display both obscene and somehow enthralling—nay, it was the tenderness involved. Even though they were going about the process like animals, the soft whispers, the sweet sighs, the gentleness of each touch, reflected something else entirely.

Could that be—

"Love," he said, the word a low, rumbling growl.

Near the pond the man tilted his head as if he'd heard, and Reginald frowned. He knew that man. It was—

No. Couldn't be. This fellow only resembled the other. Because Will Shakespeare was in London, crying over the empty bier of his dead mistress.

If Reginald could have smiled with his snout, he would have. Because Shakespeare's mistress was now at the bottom of the ocean, where no one—especially the wondrous bard—would ever see her again.

Where only a day before, that thought would have made Reginald want to dance, strangely now, it made him restless. His ear—still positioned on the side of his head, but larger, furrier, floppier—flicked.

"Must have been a fly," he murmured, continuing to watch.

A warm, strange, but oddly pleasant sensation blossomed in his chest when the man touched the woman's face, then she in turn touched his. Reginald wanted someone to touch him like that. But no one ever would.

His sigh was long and deep and—

Just a bit too loud.

The man's eyes narrowed on the dense overgrowth where Reginald crouched. Reginald pressed his new, amazing body into the ground, making himself as flat and unobtrusive as could be, then held his breath.

After only an instant, the woman murmured something unintelligible, and the man turned his attention back where it belonged—on her. However, the instant had been long enough for Reginald to recognize the face, though he'd seen it before but once.

The man did not just *look* like Will Shakespeare. He *was* Will Shakespeare.

Which was impossible, but eyes such as Reginald's did not lie.

Again, the emotions he believed he should feel at the revelation that his wife's lover did not love her, were absent. Why was he not suppressing a continued desire to dance?

Then again, having his wife cuckold Reginald for a man who was making love—and that *had* been love; it could be nothing else—to another mere days after her death was disturbing. Had Katherine loved Will Shakespeare at all? Shakespeare certainly hadn't loved her.

Another truth that should make Reginald laugh, but he did not. And not merely because the sound would alert the lovers to his presence, but Reginald did not think he could conjure up even a giggle over this situation if he had to.

And why *was* that?

Perhaps because he was unable to share the news with his wife. The only way Shakespeare's duplicity would be any fun at all would be if Reginald were the one to tell her of it.

Alas, she resided at the bottom of the ocean.

Shakespeare's new love chose that moment to sit up, and Reginald had to clap a paw over his snout to keep from shouting her name.

Katherine.

Impossible. Reginald's wife was dead. He had shut the coffin on her still, lifeless face himself. Which meant . . .

She was one of them.

Chapter Fourteen

"Hell is empty. And all the devils are here."

—*The Tempest* (Act I, scene 2)

Ariel had done as she was told. She had stilled the wind; the ships were becalmed. Even now, tiny boats made their way toward the shore.

She'd left Prospero chuckling on the beach. She hoped his mirth might get the best of him. Mayhap he would swallow his tongue.

She had felt bad enough sinking the ships and drowning the people. However, bringing them here to be eaten was worse. Drowning wasn't pleasant, but she thought it would be preferable to having one's brains devoured by the living dead.

"I must return to my diamond." She hurried along the path that led toward the center of the isle.

Certainly Ariel could have snapped her fingers, blinked her eyes—in truth she need but imagine where she wanted to go— and there she would be. But she was upset, angry at both her master and herself, horrified at what she'd done and what had been done to her, and she could not think straight.

"Who would have thought a sprite of my power would become a slave."

And though she traveled several feet above the ground so as not to dirty her silver feet, Ariel drew back her leg and made a kicking motion, gratified when a good-sized rock flew into a nearby tree and knocked it down.

Sometimes wanton destruction was most satisfying.

Though she loathed Prospero and what he had made her do, Ariel did understand deep down why he was doing it. Prospero had been as much a victim as she—torn from his home, forced to live on a deserted island, his only remaining birthright that blasted book of spells. Little wonder he was obsessed by them, and by the vengeance he would take with their results.

Or the vengeance he hoped to take. Ariel, despite any trickle of sympathy, would do her best to thwart her master's plan. But it was tricky. *She* was bound to obey him, which meant she needed someone else's help.

She believed the arrival of a *chasseur* upon a passing ship had been not serendipitous but prophetic. Ariel's cause was just; hence a zombie hunter arrived on the same wind as the zombies.

How she had known the *chasseur* resided upon the vessel was merely fairy intuition. Sometimes Ariel knew things. Not all the time, but when an insight came to her, she was never wrong. She had not been wrong about the hunter named Diamond.

Particles casted across Ariel's face, caught in her eyelashes, stuck to her neck. She lifted her hand, snatched one between two silver fingers, and stared.

Ashes. Her diamond had been busy.

Except Katherine had been at the pool with her sleeping

un-man. How had she gotten free of the thick tangle of green-ery and begun killing zombies? The zombies had certainly not had the wherewithal to make their way to her.

Ariel cursed in the language of the fairies, and distant lightning flashed. She hoped the woman hadn't hacked down all the trees.

The pool was separated from the rest of the island by a dense and near impenetrable jungle. Ariel wanted to keep it that way. No one knew about the area but her. It was the only place she could be removed for certain from the range of Prospero's beady blue eyes.

Ariel reached the point where the foliage thickened. If she wished, she could now think of the waterfall and magically be there. However, the ashes that stirred gently in the breeze con-cerned her. She wanted to see for herself that the barrier to her only paradise remained intact. So instead of transportation, Ariel murmured a few words of fairy, and her person grew small.

'Twas the Spell of the Sidhe—the Gaelic being the best way to describe Ariel and those like her. Sidhe literally meant "people of the mounds." But the legends of the Irish about the fey were the closest things to the truth Ariel had heard.

There was something about the Irish. They saw what others did not. Of course, most said this was because of their fond-ness for ale, but Ariel knew differently.

The Spell of the Sidhe made Ariel small. 'Twas how the fairy folk hid. Their true natures were tall, strong, and colorful. But as time moved on, and overly strong giants, or silver flying women, became cause for curiosity and sometimes violence, the sidhe made use of their magic to shrink. If fairies were the size of a fly, a fly was what humans saw.

Even the Irish after a while.

Ariel flitted left, right, dodging trees and shrubs, along with the occasional flake of ash. Though the flecks were light as gossamer, they were larger than her, and if she went through one, she'd be covered in it. Considering what the ash had been, Ariel avoided them like the zombie plague they once were.

The closer she came to the secluded glade, the less ash she dodged, and Ariel did not see any indication that her diamond had used a sword to free herself from the overgrowth. The place looked exactly the same now as it had a thousand times before.

But for the two people entwined upon the grassy bed at the pond's edge.

Ariel was unable to keep herself from staring. The man lay atop the woman. He stared into her face with such an intense expression, Ariel's stomach shimmied. The woman reached up, drew her fingers down the man's cheek, and the starkness of the emotion on his face caused the shimmy in Ariel's stomach to lift into her chest. She put her hand atop her breast, afraid her heart might tumble free.

Then they pressed their lips together—how odd—and kept them there for a long time. Had they become stuck?

Eventually the man lifted his head. They murmured to each other, the words difficult to make out, until the last.

"Doubt thou the stars are fire. Doubt that the sun doth move. Doubt truth to be a liar. But never doubt I love."

Love?

Ariel had heard the word in relation to Prospero's book. Oh, how he loved it.

She had declared the same herself in relation to the island. She loved living here. Would love it even more were she alone.

Ariel tilted her head as the man began to move, his body thrusting against the woman's. What *were* they doing?

The gasps and moans, the slap of flesh upon flesh. She feared he might be hurting her. Ariel nearly flew forward, but the woman met those thrusts with thrusts of her own, and the expressions upon their faces now reflected anything but pain. She thought that might be—

"Ecstasy," she whispered.

The movements increased in speed and strength. The sounds became more pained. Ariel became hot; she who was always so cool. Her hand upon her chest strayed to one breast and began to stroke. Nothing in her long life had ever caused her to feel so strange.

Her body fair tingled in places that had never tingled before. A light mist seemed to have sprung up from her very pores, causing her skin to turn full and moist. Yet, strangely, those areas that tingled, while also moist, ached to be filled.

She considered the man and the woman. Ah! He was putting something *in*to her. She must have that empty feeling too. She certainly appeared to enjoy the filling.

Suddenly the man's gaze flicked to the trees on the opposite side of the pond. The behavior was so surprising—until now all the man had seen was his woman—that Ariel looked too. She saw nothing, and he must not have either because when the diamond pulled his attention back to her, he gave it gladly.

The two stilled, even their very breath, though now that she considered it, Ariel had not heard the man breathe, nor seen the rise and fall of his chest, though Katherine's breasts fair jiggled with the force of her own panting.

Her diamond had said the man would not become a zombie, and Ariel could see that he had not. However, there was something about him that bothered her. But right now she was too curious over what they were doing to examine the feeling further.

The man fell to his back on the grass, keeping his legs, his fingers, entangled with Katherine's. They did not speak, but still he seemed so sad.

Mayhap he *had* seen something in the jungle. Ariel lifted her gaze, and then *she* did not breathe.

Caliban rose from the rushes like a vengeful pagan god. His upper lip lifted in loathing and fury darkened his eyes as he rushed forward. Though he was only half wolf, no one would have known it by his appearance. As he bore down on the oblivious lovers, sharp teeth dripping, claws bared, he was all ravenous beast bent on murder.

Ariel flew across the pond, skimming the surface of the water so closely the back spray caused by her speed cooled her overly warm body. She cleared the still reclining man and woman—she thought the man might even have seen her, something no "man" could have done—and wished them away, even as she flicked one hand at the great blond creature.

The next instant Ariel stood on a mountaintop, staring at the distant puff of greenery where she had so recently been.

She turned toward the approaching thump of paws. "What were you—"

The rest of the question became but a gurgle as his claw tore through her throat.

Chapter Fifteen

"But one fiend at a time."
—*The Tempest* (Act III, scene 3)

"What was—" Will began, then blinked.

I could do nothing but the same. We had been tangled together on the grassy bank of the waterfall-fed pool.

Now sand scratched my shoulders, seabirds circled above, and the crash of the ocean made Will's next words indistinguishable.

I sat up, wincing as sand ground into places sand should not be. Will leaped to his feet, nearly falling onto his face as his breeches encircled his ankles. He yanked them into place and held out a hand to me.

His lifted brow indicated his words had been a question I had not answered. I shook my head, tapped my ear. So he raised his voice and tried again. "Did you see her?"

I repeated the shaking of my head.

"A tiny, silver woman flew above us and then—" He indicated the beach.

"Ariel." Was she invisible to humans or merely to me?

"She was not so small before."

"If she can move us hither and yon, as well as bring the storm, I doubt shrinking causes her any difficulty."

"Why here?" Will asked.

Not a dead body in sight—reclining or shambling. All that resided on this beach were shells, dead fish, and us.

"God's elbow," I muttered. "My sword."

That still lay near the pool.

"Ariel!" I tilted my head and listened. All I heard were the waves, so I stood and moved to the edge of the jungle. "Ariel!"

No response. Unless you counted the distant scream.

I was running before I even thought. Zombies do not scream. Therefore, someone needed me.

Will appeared at my side. He scooped me off my feet. I had to close my eyes or become ill as the trees flew backward at a dizzying speed. When he stopped, the jolt made me gasp.

"Shh," he murmured, gaze narrowed.

I saw nothing. However, when I listened, another sound had replaced the screams.

The distinct cacophony of eating.

I struggled, and Will set me down, then together we crept forward until we could peek through the foliage.

Zombies were everywhere. Each one appeared to have his own banquet of brains.

Will caught my elbow as I advanced, spinning me around. I opened my mouth, and he put a finger to his. Then he drew me away where we would not be heard, although from the volume of the chomping and tearing, the lip smacking and teeth gnashing, we could have spoken right there and never been noticed.

"They have killed a dozen people."

"If I let you go, you will be next." Will brushed my hair from my face. "Kate, you do not have a sword."

And without it, I was useless.

"But—" I turned toward the continuing yummy noises. "I can't just let them walk away."

"I will go." He put his hands on my shoulders. "You will stay. No matter what you hear, you will not follow. Promise me."

I hesitated. Will was very hard to kill. But he *could* die.

I didn't want him to go. I had just gotten him back. I wanted never to let him out of my sight again. But what choice did I have? There were now people on the island.

How? Why? When? All questions that must be answered, but not now.

"All right," I agreed, though it pained me. "But Will, I cannot—" I broke off, horrified when my eyes began to burn with tears. "I cannot watch you die. If things go badly, I will come to you."

"No," he said.

I had a sudden premonition, and I shivered. "Oh God, I have an ill-divining soul! Methinks I see thee as one dead in the bottom of a tomb." I set my hand upon his dear face. "Either my eyesight fails, or thou look'st pale."

His lips curved, those cool, luscious lips I had so recently kissed, and he set his palm atop mine. "I am forever pale."

Annoyance flared, and I withdrew my hand. "I do not want to live if you are dead."

"Sweet Kate, I have been dead for centuries."

"Undead is not dead."

"It is certainly not alive," he muttered.

I frowned. When had he started to believe that?

Will pushed through the foliage and into the clearing. I expected the eating sounds to cease, but they did not. I crept closer until I could see everything.

The *tibonage* must have been starving, for they did not even glance up when Will placed his beautiful hands on each side of the nearest fiend's head and twisted. For an instant, surprise widened the creature's eyes, then the expression fell away as did he. Ashes scattered over the open, bloody skull of his victim like salt.

Will moved fast, becoming nigh onto a blur as he stepped from zombie to zombie doing the same thing—grasp, twist, and move on. Why had the man ever bothered with a sword?

"To appear human," I murmured. In London, he must behave like everyone else. But here, he could be what he was. An exceptional killer. That he killed what was already dead did not lessen in any way his talent at doing so.

Perhaps I should have been disgusted; instead I merely wished I could kill them like that.

Will had very little trouble turning every zombie in the clearing to ash. The last two noticed something amiss before he reached them and lumbered to their feet, murmuring: "Brr?"

I surged forward as one came at him from the front, another from the back. Will cast me a glare—his superior hearing had alerted him to my movement—and dispatched them with embarrassing ease. He simply backhanded one, and while the creature was stumbling, its feet stepping on its own toes, he tore the head off the other. Before the first had managed to untangle itself, Will had finished it too.

I couldn't help it. I began to clap. "Bravo! Encore!"

My chest went hot and thick in response to Will's brilliant smile. It always did. He was the most beautiful man I had ever known—both inside and out. He would say he was not a man but a fiend. I knew differently. It took more than breathing to make someone human.

My gaze on Will, my heart fair dancing with love for him, I did not watch my feet. As I ran to him, I slid in the blood, or perhaps it was the brains, and began to fall.

Will was at my side in an instant, snatching my elbow to prevent me from wallowing in muck. His smile faded as he took in the destruction. "I told you not to watch," he snapped.

"You told me not to follow," I corrected. "And if you recall the conversation, I did not agree."

He continued to look away; he did not respond. I tried to turn his face back to me, but he would not allow it. "Will?"

"Do not look at me now," he whispered. "Do not see me like this."

"Like what?"

"My fangs," he managed. "They are out."

I thought back to his smile, how beautiful I had thought it, and realized something. "I did not even notice."

His gaze flicked to mine then away. I moved in close, framed his face, kissed his lips without fear, held on when he would have flinched away. "Do not ever hide from me what you are. I love you, Will. All of you. Everything. For always."

"You do not know all that I have done."

I released him. "I do not care."

He opened his mouth to reply then turned his attention sharply to the rear. "Someone is coming."

My hand went to my hip, and my teeth ground together in frustration. I was not used to being without a sword.

"Stay out of sight." Will herded me toward the opening in the greenery that I had come through.

I was also not used to being protected. I was usually the one doing the defending. I found I did not like the turnabout, and hung back.

"Kate," Will said urgently. "Mayhap it is more of them."

Most likely it was more of them.

I fought the urge to throw myself in front of him regardless of my lack of sword. As much as I disliked the fact, my remaining in view would only hamper Will's ability to deal with the *tibonage*.

I slid through the gap and ducked just as a large man—both tall and wide—wearing ancient, dusty robes strode into the clearing. Beneath one arm he carried a book that appeared older than both his robes and his person.

He turned left, then right, causing his long red-and-white hair to twirl out from his head like a fan. "Who did this?" he roared. "Who killed my risen dead? Who dares?"

He was the one whom Ariel had promised. *He* had ordered her to kill. Was he also the one who had raised the zombies? He did not look like a vampire. Then again, neither had Will.

"I do," Will said.

It was as if the man were seeing Will for the first time, even though Will had been there all along. He stiffened, blue gaze widening. "How came you here and breathing?"

Will opened his mouth, perhaps to mention that he did not breathe, then, apparently, thought better of it.

At Will's lack of response, the newcomer's face reddened further. He drew himself up, towering over Will; he must have outweighed him by at least three stone. If he was merely a man, this did not matter. On the other hand, if he were a necro-vampire—

Instead of attacking, snatching out Will's throat with one

hand, or, perhaps, growing fangs, the old man pulled free his book, opened it, and paged through.

"Who are you, sir?" Will asked. "How came you here? Why do you raise the dead?"

"Be silent, knave! Can you not see that I am busy?"

The fellow spoke as if he were a king, and mayhap he was. King of this island. Lord of the zombies. Ruler of all he surveyed.

Or so he thought.

"Ah, here it is." He poked a finger as thick as a Polonian sawsedge at the page then began to mutter.

I could catch only a few words—poisonous slave, devil, wicked—it did not sound good. Then he poked the sawsedge finger at Will's face and announced, "Beasts shall tremble at thy din."

Will's eyes crossed as he stared at the appendage hovering so close to the end of his nose.

The old man scowled. "A caliban you are!" Now he actually tapped Will once, sharply between the eyes. When nothing happened, he pulled the finger back and squinted at it, shook the hand frantically, then pointed it again. "Half man, half monster. Behold!"

Will continued to stare at him most calmly.

The fellow held up the book like a shield then peeked around it. "What *are* you?"

"What are *you*?" Will returned, then snatched the book from the old fool's hands so quickly he was left standing there with his fingers yet curled about nothing.

"Demon!" he shouted, though Will was close enough to hear a whisper. "Return that at once."

Will snorted and began to page through. His amusement

quickly died at what he found there. He lifted his gaze. "Where did you get this?"

"It is mine."

"And you are?"

"Prospero."

"A sorcerer," Will said.

The old man muttered words Kate could not understand then curled his fingers in a *come to me* gesture. The book flew from Will's hands to land once again in his. "And a king who will soon take back his throne."

Chapter Sixteen

"Wipe thou thine eyes; have comfort."

—*The Tempest* (Act I, scene 2)

Reginald's claw sliced through Ariel's throat before he could stop it. Her voice became a gurgle, and her head tilted slowly sideways.

"I'm sorry," he barked. But sorry would not keep her head upon her shoulders now that he had chopped it off.

The rapier slice shone dark pewter against the silver sheen of her skin. It went all the way through her neck; her head should have tumbled right off. Her body should have turned to ashes before her noggin reached the ground.

Instead, Ariel rolled her eyes in disgust, grabbed her skull, yanked it back into place, settled the appendage with a firm, downward motion, then dropped her arms. Within seconds, the thin dark line faded and disappeared.

"What—? How—?" Reginald lifted his gaze to hers. "Huh?"

"I am a fairy." She dusted off her hands. "Such would not kill me."

"What would?"

Now she stared down her pert, silver nose. "You think I would tell you and die?"

"I would not hurt you."

"You just did."

"But you said—"

"I said that would not kill me. I did not say it did not hurt."

"I'm sorry," he repeated, and he was. He had never had a beautiful woman treat him as a man. Perhaps this was because Ariel was not a woman, and he was no longer merely a man. Nevertheless, he liked it and her. "I did not wish to kill you, but the zombie—"

"Thou dost believe?"

He turned his gaze to the island far below. Beautiful it was— all the possibilities of green and brown, with dots of red, orange, yellow, surrounded by an unearthly, unending blue. 'Twould be paradise, except here and there the trees shivered, revealing the location of creatures more suited to hell.

"I have seen."

"Seeing goes a long way toward believing," she agreed. "But there were no zombies at the pool."

"My wife, she—"

"Ah!" Ariel laid her hand upon his furry arm; mayhap 'twas now more a leg. "That explains much."

"About what?"

"I cast my spell to save the diamond. As you were there, and a diamond as well, you were spared."

Reginald considered what she was saying. For some reason Ariel had wanted to save Katherine, knew her name was Dymond, and had performed magic, but—

"Why?" he asked.

"I needed a *chasseur*."

"A what?"

"Hunter."

"I do not hunt," he said. He had never possessed the stomach for it.

Until today, when his stomach had become as altered as his hands.

"You were not the *chasseur*, nor the diamond, I did seek."

"Katherine?" Reginald began to laugh, the sound reminiscent of the annoying yip of a lapdog. Reginald forced himself to stop, clear his throat, and continue. "My wife is not a hunter. She does not even much care for the taste of meat."

Unless it is Shakespeare's, murmured an evil little voice in his head.

'Twas Ariel's turn to laugh, though hers sounded like the tinkling of tiny bells on a warm summer breeze. Reginald could have listened to it forever.

"Your wife is one of the greatest zombie hunters alive."

"That's ..." He paused before the word *impossible* slipped free. Because it was, of course, *not* impossible. In truth, if he inserted the idea of his wife as a zombie hunter into the explanation of many strange things, they became not so strange at all.

Except for how she came to be alive on this island after he had placed her dead within a coffin.

"That's what?" Ariel asked, bright blue gaze fixed upon him.

"Interesting," he finished.

"You did not know?"

"We did not spend much time together. I have a plantation in the New World. She lives in the Old."

"There is a new world?" Her perfect brow creased. "Above us in the sky? Below beneath the sea?"

"No." He waved a paw to indicate the west. "It is across the ocean."

"Oh, that!" She smiled indulgently. "It is not so very new."

"You have been other places?"

"Many." She spread her arms in a graceful movement to indicate the island and all that lay upon it. "But here is the only place I wish to be."

A mere day past, Reginald would not have understood. He would have been frantic to get off this island by any means, fair or foul, to return to England, or even to Virginia, it would have mattered not. But now . . .

He was in no great hurry.

"How did the *chasseur* kill those zombies?" Ariel's beautiful silver face appeared confused. "She did not leave the pool."

"She did not kill them." Reginald stuck out his chest, which, while covered with fur, still appeared more impressive than the chest with which he had been born. "I did."

"You?" Her gaze swept from snout to tail. "But you are not a *chasseur*."

He wiggled his claws, and their sharp points caught the sun like diamonds. "I am now."

Understanding replaced her confusion; pleasure replaced understanding. "Two hunters with a single spell. My cause *is* just."

"What cause?"

"To kill all the zombies on this isle."

Something tickled in Reginald's brain. "But you brought the dead here so Prospero could raise them."

"Aye," she agreed.

"Yet you want them eliminated?"

"They are evil, horrible creatures."

"Then why contribute to the making of them?"

Her breasts rose and fell on a sigh. How strange that she could stand here, naked before him, and while Reginald thought her lovely, he did not find her nakedness odd but, instead, just right. When it came down to it, he was naked too, and that felt more right than anything had ever felt in his life.

"Prospero released me from the bondage cast upon me by the wicked witch Sycorax."

"There's a witch?" Reginald's voice lifted on the last word until it resembled a startled yip. He had forever been afraid of them. Most likely because of some long forgotten tale whispered to his childhood self right before bedtime. Why did people *do* that?

Ariel shook her head. "There is a witch no longer."

"Just a sorcerer, a fairy, and the zombies."

"Do not forget the caliban."

How could he?

"I pledged to do his bidding."

"And he bids you to kill?"

Her shoulders slumped. "He does."

"So you do as he asks, then you bring a hunter to thwart him." Reginald tried to grin, but all he could do was open his snout and let his tongue loll free. "'Tis most clever."

Ariel's head came up. "You think so?"

"I do," he agreed. "Why is he raising the dead?"

Ariel's gaze returned to the distant trees, and her brow wrinkled again. "He requires a zombie army to take back his throne."

"What throne?"

"I did not ask."

Reginald would have thought that would be the first question asked, but maybe not by a fairy, who cared little for worldly things. Then again, from what Reginald had observed of Prospero, the man was far from sane. The old fool might have imagined everything, making any question about his throne moot.

Silence fell between them, broken now and then by the distant shriek of a bird, which to Reginald sounded quite human. But according to what Ariel had told him, the only non-zombies upon the island were the diamonds she had saved, Prospero, herself, and—

As if she heard his thoughts, Ariel blurted: "How came the other man here?"

"Shakespeare?" The name rumbled out on a snarl.

"He is not another diamond?"

"He is a common playwright. My wife's . . ." His lip lifted. "Lover."

"I do not understand this word. Should not your wife love you?"

Reginald shrugged. He had pretended to love Katherine to convince her to marry him, but he was not certain he *could* love. For all the pretty words of poets—words he had spewed himself to get what he wanted—Reginald wasn't sure the emotion existed. He had never seen evidence of it.

His parents' marriage had been arranged. They barely spoke to each other, let alone spouted of love. They barely tolerated Reginald.

The only time his father had ever looked upon him with anything akin to kindness was on Reginald's wedding day. And then only because he'd done what he'd been told, and well. He'd wooed the wealthy merchant's daughter, winning both her and her sizable dowry with the love-words as his father had instructed him.

According to his bride's father—who'd desired the marriage in order that Reginald's good and ancient name would take away the taint of earned money from his own—his daughter had a soft spot for poetry and the theater.

Reginald hadn't realized until later just what that soft spot was.

Damn Shakespeare, who mooned about and spoke of love; he made his living off it. But love was as easily lost as won, and if that was so, then had it truly been love at all?

"We did not marry for love," he admitted.

"Then why should she not love another?"

Reginald frowned. "It is . . ." He paused. He had been about to say "not done," but that was a lie. It was done quite often; however, most adulterers made less a spectacle of themselves than his not-quite-dead-enough wife.

"This Shakespeare," Ariel continued, ignoring Reginald's unfinished answer. "What is he?"

"A playwright," Reginald repeated. "That means—"

She lifted a silvery palm. "I know what a playwright is. I meant what *is* he? He cannot be human."

Reginald stifled another laugh. He'd laughed at the existence of zombies then spent the morning killing them. He'd chuckled at the idea of his wife as a zombie hunter, but she was. Amusement over the inhumanity of Will Shakespeare would only be a waste of time.

"I do not know what he is," Reginald admitted.

"When you sliced off my head, you meant to slice off his," she mused.

"No," Reginald said. "'Twas hers I was after."

"You hate her that much?"

"I thought she was one of them."

"A zombie?" Ariel's stunning blue eyes widened. "Why?"

"The last time I saw my dear wife," Reginald said, "she was lying dead in her coffin."

Chapter Seventeen

"What's past is prologue."
—*The Tempest* (Act II, scene I)

"Of all the islands, in all the oceans, in all the world," Will muttered, "he walked onto mine."

"What say you?" Prospero asked.

"Plots. Dialogue." Will flapped his hand. "'Tis nothing."

But it *was* something. A looming war. A distant, exotic shore. A tavern with a sad-eyed man. A beautiful woman the man had known before and a song about time passing by.

"Thou art insane."

"Pot. Kettle," Will murmured, trying to bring back the idea, but it was gone.

At least they'd had Paris, he thought. Whatever that meant. Such was the way with his imagination. Sometimes a concept would appear, at others he would hear people speaking; he would catch hints of their background or flickers of their future. Then, someone would hail him from the real world, and all that he had imagined would be gone.

Poof.

But the best ideas returned. Usually.

"Will! Psst!"

Just like the ghosts that constantly called his name.

He caught sight of a face peering at him from the trees—Kate, not a ghost—and frowned, shook his head, glanced at Prospero. He did not want the crazy old man with his book of spells that could do God only knew what to lay eyes on Kate. Ever.

However Prospero was either hard of hearing or too involved in his next bit of mischief to notice, perhaps both, for he had shoved his nose back in the book.

The man was mad, although . . .

In most of Will's plays 'twas the fools and the madmen who told the truth.

Will narrowed his gaze upon the tome. Prospero had called the thing to him with a mere flick of one hand. By his own admission, he had raised zombies. He was not a necro-vampire; Will would know. Therefore the fellow had used a magic spell. He *was* a sorcerer, as he had claimed.

But that did not make him king.

Yet.

Will suddenly understood the reason for the zombie army.

"I say." Will took a step forward, looking into the man's eyes, giving him a little push. "What throne are you after?"

Instead of answering, Prospero tossed something at Will's feet. There was a *pop,* a blaze of fire, then smoke, and when it cleared, the old man had disappeared.

"A pox upon thee," Will muttered. Pointless, since Prospero was gone and could no doubt cure the pox if it ever came upon him.

That was neither here nor there. What concerned Will now was that the man had ignored his "push." He had never before come across anyone who could. Of course, he had never before met a sorcerer.

Kate emerged from the trees. Will lifted a brow. "You heard?"

"Aye," she agreed. "Sorcerer. Zombie raiser. King with a lost throne. Blah, blah, blah."

"Blah?" Will repeated. He had not heard the word before.

"I made it up. It means 'and so on, and so forth, into eternity, I care not.'"

"Hmm." Will enjoyed making up words. He did so quite often.

For instance, he had coined the word *zany* in a play he had begun not long ago. 'Twas an amusing word and sounded like what it meant—clowning, buffoonery, and the like. Will called the play *Love's Work Misplaced*. If he could but think of a better title, he might even allow his creation to be performed.

Will decided he quite liked blah, blah, blah. It saved so much time and said many things while at the same time saying nothing at all.

"Will?" Kate touched his arm, and he peered into her face.

His love for her hit him so hard he thought his heart might begin to beat again. What had he done to deserve such joy? Even trapped on an island with zombies he was happier than he could ever remember being in all his lifetimes.

Will kissed her. He could not help himself. And Kate kissed him back, tangling her fingers in his hair, running her thumb along the hoop in his ear. Whenever she did that, his body responded like the man he had once been. The man he sometimes wished he could be again. For her.

"Stop." She laid her palm against his chest and stepped back. She knew him so well. For the instant she moved away, he could not help but follow. His Kate called to him like a siren upon the sea.

Her eyes glazed, her face flushed, she tasted of red wine, and she smelled of roses—flavors both familiar and forever exotic.

"Not here," she whispered. "Not now. I called you for a reason."

Will. Psst! Ah, yes.

He took her hand in his, lifting it from his chest, where her warmth burned against his eternal chill. "What is amiss?"

He rubbed a thumb along her palm, and her lips parted; her tongue darted out. "I . . . uh . . ."

The vein in her neck throbbed. He could not draw his gaze away from that pulsing skein of life.

"Stop," she repeated, and withdrew her hand. "I cannot think when you touch me."

The complete opposite of him. When she touched him thoughts tumbled through his mind like small rocks along the bed of a flooded stream.

"How can my muse want subject to invent while thou dost breathe," he murmured.

Her lips curved, and more words gushed in.

"Teach not thy lip such scorn, for it was made for kissing, lady."

She laughed. "You cannot woo me with pretty words, Will Shakespeare."

"Methinks I have before."

"Save them. But now . . ." Her laughter died, and she turned to the jungle. "I heard more screams."

All the words in his head disappeared in the face of just one. "Where?" She pointed, and he swept out one arm. "Lead on, Macduff."

"Who is Macduff?"

Will was not certain where the phrase had come from, but he liked it, and he knew where it should go. "I have been thinking of a play set in Scotland. There was a king there long ago; to history he is an able man, an excellent ruler by the name of Macbeth. They called him the Red King."

"You knew him?" she asked, and began to lead on as he'd instructed, shoving aside the dense foliage that hampered their way.

"I did. He was not the man that history has indicated."

Kate glanced over her shoulder with lifted brows. "You made him a zombie army?"

Will shrugged. He had made armies for lesser kings than Macbeth.

"He was consumed by ambition—a great soldier, a natural leader. He would have become king without the zombie army if he'd only had some patience. But his wife . . ." Will paused. "She was such a witch."

"An actual witch?"

"No." If she had been, there would have been no need for Will's help. "I was being polite. She was a coldhearted bitch."

However, Kate's question made him consider . . . A witch, or three, could be an interesting addition to the plot.

"Double, double toil and trouble; fire burn, and cauldron bubble," he murmured.

"You do love to rhyme, Will Shakespeare."

His mind cleared a bit and he smiled. "Rhymes intrigue people. Or mayhap they are just more easily remembered. Those lines in my plays that rhyme are often the ones bandied about the most. And the more a playwright is quoted, the more famous he becomes."

"I believe you will be quite famous," Kate said. "People will be quoting your plays centuries from now."

Considering that Will would still be *alive* centuries from now, he'd make sure of it.

"*Lay* on, Macduff," he muttered.

"What?" Kate stopped, and Will crashed into her. He had to snatch her waist to keep her from falling. Then her lovely, round, barely clothed rump pressed into his crotch, and for a minute he forgot what he'd said.

She turned, and her breasts brushed his arm. His fangs began to itch. "I ... uh ..."

His gaze was drawn to her décolletage. He'd seen women's breasts displayed amid velvet, silk, and gold, but nothing had ever been more beautiful than Kate's breasts framed by torn, dirty linen, with a sheen of sparkling perspiration on top. Only Kate could sparkle like that. He wanted to lick the moisture free, perhaps—

She snapped her fingers in front of his nose. "I'm up here."

His gaze lifted, and his mind cleared, though his teeth did not stop itching. "The phrase should be '*Lay* on, Macduff,' not 'Lead on.'"

"Because?"

"'Lay on' is an invitation to violence. 'Lead on' would indicate compliance. And I believe Macduff will see the true nature of Macbeth."

"He is you."

Will's brows lifted. "Me?"

"Is there not a character in each play who speaks with your voice?"

Will considered. He *had* put much of his own thoughts into the words of Armado in *Love's Work Misplaced*. And though Valentine in *Two Gentlemen of Verona* had been a real person, some-one Will had killed long ago who haunted him until he'd agreed to tell the man's story, Will had done so by adding to the manu-script many of his own beliefs and sly cuts at the world in which they lived. 'Twas what he did.

"You are the most brilliant of women." Will kissed Kate's cheek, became lured by the curve of that cheek into her jaw and then her neck. He pressed kisses to them all. "Beautiful and tal-ented as well."

"Mmm," she agreed. "Go on."

"Lustrous." 'Twas one of his own words—a favorite.

He pressed his mouth to a ripe swell, licked it too, and her breath caught. More of his creations flowed free. "Radiant." She arched, offering him herself. "Arousing."

Then another scream split the air, and Kate straightened so fast they nearly bumped heads. She turned, set to rush head-long into danger, as was her way, and Will caught her wrist, spinning her back into his arms.

"Will." She struggled. "Someone is dying."

"Someone will always be dying, sweet Kate. But once again, you have not a sword. I will go first."

Her lips tightened. 'Twas not her nature to hang back, to follow. But she nodded. "Lead on, Macduff," she repeated.

He had a feeling that phrase was going to become popular, even though 'twould not be the correct one.

Will traveled forward, Kate's hand in his. He wished he could walk everywhere like this for the rest of his—nay, make that *her* life. With Kate's warmth to counter his chill, he felt he could do anything.

Then, suddenly, her hand was snatched away. Will spun, ready to argue. She no doubt wanted to insist that she lead.

The sight that met his eyes caused his teeth to click together then grind a bit.

"Brr," said the zombie, his own teeth clacking far too close to Kate's neck.

The festering fiend clasped her in his arms. She had stretched as far from his searching jaws as she could get, but the creature held on tight.

Seeing his love in the embrace of a monster caused Will's own monster to flare free. His fangs sprouted, cutting his lips. The blood that flowed into his mouth only made him wish to roar. So he did.

The zombie lifted his head. "Brrr?" he asked, an instant before Will snatched that head off.

Kate had been straining so hard in the opposite direction that when the arms of the thing that had captured her turned to ash, she fell. The rest of the creature descended slowly, like fat, gray drops of rain, sprinkling over her face, landing in her hair, sticking to her eyelashes.

Will bent to assist her, but before he could, something hit him from behind, and instead he sprawled upon her.

"Umph," she said as he landed on her stomach.

Pain erupted in Will's ankle. He kicked with his other foot and was rewarded with a muffled "Brrumph," a thud, and a cessation of the immediate agony, though the area did continue to throb.

He had been bitten! But better him than Kate. The bite of a zombie would be nothing more than a discomfort to Will; for Kate it would be death.

A zombie's rotting mouth was poison. Once bitten, a human would die within days. But contrary to popular legend, the afflicted would not rise again by virtue of the bite. Only a necro-vampire—or, apparently, a sorcerer's spell—could do that.

Will rolled free, taking an instant to make certain no other fiends had crept up on their flank. None had. Still, they were surrounded by jungle. No wall to set their back against. He hated that.

"Will!" she shouted, pointing over his shoulder.

He spun, jerked back, avoiding the snap of zombie teeth upon the end of his nose. He backhanded the creature, and it flew into the six that stood behind it, knocking them down like skittle pins. Several more emerged from the trees, and Kate's horrified gasp only infuriated him.

No one would hurt her while he was here.

The scent of blood—the zombies had been busy; they were drenched in it—called to Will's beast. His fangs were already out so he gave himself over to the monster within.

He mowed through the advancing creatures, using both hands and teeth. Ashes sprayed; the air thickened with them. He lost count of how many he killed; he only knew that he must destroy every one to save her.

When at last no more emerged from the trees, no further rumbles of "brrr!" haunted the wind, Will sank to his knees, allowing the remains of the creatures that tumbled past to sift through his filthy fingers.

His ankle burned; he cast a disinterested glance in its direction. The flesh was torn, bleeding. But he would not need to concern himself that it would fester. Certainly it would sting, and without human blood it would take a long time to heal, but Will Shakespeare need never again worry about death by gangrene.

One less thing.

The sound of heavy breathing filled the now silent air. 'Twas not Will. So it must be Kate.

Was she horrified by his violence? Scarred by the sight of him as monster? Near tears to think that she had touched such a creature as he with love?

He did not want to face her. He was covered in grit and gore, his fangs yet out; he'd even bloodied his lip. But he must. He had learned over his long lives that it was best just to get these things done.

Will lifted his gaze, bracing himself for what he would see in hers.

Kate's eyes were wide but not with fear. Her face was pale but not with horror. Her lips were parted but not in preparation to scream. Instead, he could have sworn her expression was one of admiration.

"Kate?" he managed, his voice but a whisper that shook.

"Sometimes I wonder, Will Shakespeare." She crossed the short distance between them, bothered not at all by the zombie ash that casted over her bare feet.

She brushed his hair back from his face then leaned down and kissed him directly on the mouth, ignoring, or mayhap not caring, just where that mouth had been.

"Why did you ever bother with a sword?"

Chapter Eighteen

"For some of you there present are worse than devils."

—*The Tempest* (Act III, scene 3)

"I told you he was not human."

Ariel and Caliban peeked through the fronds at the carnage taking place in the clearing.

After hearing Caliban's pronouncement of his wife's death, Ariel had wished them to wherever Katherine resided—she wanted the truth of this—waved her hand, and they were there.

Unfortunately, so were the zombies.

But not for long. Will Shakespeare made short work of the shambling horrors while Ariel, Caliban, and the greatest living *chasseur* in all the land but watched.

"You are sure he is not a diamond?" Ariel asked as the unman tore off yet another head with little effort at all.

"I am sure," Caliban growled, eyes gleaming with hatred.

Ariel did not understand his dislike of Shakespeare. If Caliban did not care for his wife, what did it matter if someone else did? Humans were forever an odd, yet intriguing, race.

"If he were, 'twould explain how he came to walk upon this isle," she mused. But if he was not a diamond, he was not. There had to be another explanation for Shakespeare to be here and not at the bottom of the sea. "I wonder if he is the reason your wife is no longer dead."

Caliban's ears perked. "How so?"

"If he has access to magicks, he could do most anything."

"Magicks," Caliban rumbled. "Like your master?"

"Mayhap. Though my master's powers come from the spells within his book, some"—Ariel flipped her hands outward—"like me, are born that way."

Shakespeare tore the head off the last zombie. He stood amid a gray pile of death then slowly sank to his knees. How strange. He'd seemed energized while he killed them, but now that he was victorious he appeared defeated.

Then he turned, and Ariel understood how he had come to be here at all. "No wonder he survived drowning," she murmured.

"Why?"

Caliban stared at Ariel and not at Shakespeare. She jabbed a finger; his gaze followed then widened. "Are those . . . fangs?"

"He is a vampire."

Caliban roared, "A wh—"

Ariel waved one hand, and he finished his far-too-loud question upon a distant beach.

"—at?"

"You heard me very well."

"There is no such thing as a vampire."

"This from a man who appears half wolf."

He tilted his head in a gesture very much like that of a wolf. "He was bespelled?"

"No." Ariel considered what she knew of vampires. As she

was an ancient being, she had encountered a few. "Vampires are made by other vampires."

"Not all."

"Aye," she corrected. "All."

"There had to have been a first."

Ariel's brows lifted, and she smiled at Caliban then ran her palm gently across his snout. "You are right. How clever of you."

He blinked, jerking back in surprise. "I ... uh ... have never been called that before."

"I cannot understand why."

He slid his head closer. "Touch me again."

She patted him on the head and continued. "The identity of the first vampire is not important. I doubt it was Shakespeare. Even if it was, that matters not. What matters is that he is here, and he is an excellent hunter."

Caliban straightened. "*I* am an excellent hunter!"

"You will never be as good as him." A snarl rippled from Caliban's mouth. "Stop that," she said absently, and he did. "Shakespeare is dangerous. Violent, vicious, and very hard to kill."

"As am I," Caliban muttered.

She ignored him. "At least it explains why he is alive ..." She paused. "Well, not *alive,* because he is not, but walking and talking, on the island."

"Why?" Caliban asked, his voice just short of a growl.

"He does not breathe; therefore he cannot drown."

"How came he here?"

"Mayhap he walked."

"On water, no doubt," he muttered.

"Through it, most like. I have never heard of a vampire walking upon it."

Caliban's lip lifted in a sneer, or perhaps a snarl. "I meant how came he to be on the very next ship as I and the body of my *sainted* wife? I told no one but those who sailed with me that I had brought her."

"How indeed?" Ariel tapped a silver finger against her silver lips, causing sparks to erupt hither and yon. "I would like to know the answer to that as well."

She lifted her hand, prepared to discover the truth immediately, and Caliban reached for her arm. As he no longer had fingers but claws, one sliced through her flesh.

Ariel hissed in pain; he cringed. "I'm sorry!"

She cast him an evil glance. Being cut hurt; she did not enjoy it, but wait a moment and it would fade away.

Ariel stared at the charcoal line on her forearm, which burned like fire but became slowly less painful and less visible until neither pain, nor slice, existed any longer.

"Why did you do that?" she asked.

"I . . ." He glanced down. "I did not want you to go."

Ariel was nonplussed. No one had ever before cared if she stayed or if she went. Unless she was staying or going in order to do something for them. The idea that anyone would want her to stay because—

"Why did you want me to stay?"

He lifted his gaze. "You waved your hand and we went from there . . ." His claw, which came perilously close to her nose, indicated the jungle. "To here."

"Aye."

"Can you send me back to England in the same manner?"

Her heart, which had lightened at the idea he wanted her here because he wanted *her,* now became heavy at the realization that again she was wanted only because of what she could do.

"Nay."

"You are certain?"

Ariel thought of the occasions when she had tried to transport Prospero from this place— she would have liked nothing better than to have him gone—but such attempts on both his part and hers had resulted only in Ariel needing to rescue him from the deep.

She could leave once Prospero released her, because she could fly, though she did not wish to. However, humans—even half humans—were another matter entirely.

"I am certain," she said.

Caliban did not appear upset by this news. Instead, he seemed content. Then again, her understanding of emotions had forever been lacking.

He turned to the sea. "There is another reason I desired you here."

Ariel sighed. What would he ask for? Gold? Castles? Power? A release from the bondage of his wolf?

She waited, her foot impatiently tapping empty air.

"I . . ." He paused, and his shoulders slumped.

"You?" she repeated, the word clipped and impatient. Human requests always began with "I."

"I wanted you to touch me again." Ariel stilled. "No one has ever touched me like you did."

Chapter Nineteen

"They vanish'd strangely."

—*The Tempest* (Act III, scene 3)

Will Shakespeare amazed me.

How could he go from touching me with a passionate gentleness to tearing the heads from fetid fiends in the very next breath?

He would say because he had no breath; that he was a monster the same as they. But I did not believe it. How could I, when the love he felt for me filled his eyes?

"Kate." He set his hand on my shoulder when I would have leaned in and kissed him again. I would have kissed him forever if he would but let me. "I am unclean."

"I do not care."

"I do." He got to his feet, and it was then I noticed he'd been bitten.

"Will! Your ankle!"

He did not even glance down. "'Tis nothing."

It definitely looked like something, bloody and mangled. But he did not limp when he moved, and I knew from past experience that only the morning sun shining on his person or a sword through his throat would truly harm him. I could offer him my blood to heal more quickly, but he would not take it.

Will stared about the clearing as if he might find something he had lost. But the only thing left here was us. Even the remains of the zombies had drifted away.

"I wish I knew the location of that waterfall."

As did I. I would have liked nothing better than to be there again with him alone.

"Ariel!" I shouted.

"She did not come last time," he murmured. "I do not think she can hear anyone from afar but her master."

I thought so too. But it never hurt to try.

"The sun is fading."

I had now been awake for a night and a day, yet I did not feel tired. Mayhap the elixir Will had given me, which had caused me to sleep like the dead for two-and-forty hours, was the culprit. Or mayhap this island was a place out of time and sleep was unnecessary. Or, most likely, Ariel had gifted me with wakefulness so I could do her bidding without the encumbrance of slumber. Whatever the reason, sleep eluded me.

"Let us hie to the sea." I reached for Will's hand, but his did not meet mine halfway. I could not recall the last time that had happened. So I took his chill appendage between mine own. "We will wash free the filth of our labors."

"Labors," he murmured. "'Tis a good word."

I peered into his face. Had he gone off in his head writing? Or was this something else? I could not tell.

He allowed me to lead him from the clearing, through the jungle, and to the edge of the sea. However, when I began to undress him, he showed a bit of life.

"Kate." He stepped back. "We will be naked."

"Who would see?" I spread my hand toward the fading sun, the rolling waves, the now silent jungle. "A sprite? Her master?"

"There are zombies."

"I think there are not any longer." I reached again for his doublet. He again stepped back. What was *wrong* with him?

"There is . . ." He seemed to search for a word. How unlike him. "Their food."

Considering the amount of blood on the *tibonage,* the screams before we'd been accosted, and the silence since—

"I do not think there is any of that any longer either."

His mouth twisted. His fangs had disappeared. I quite missed them.

"I care not who sees." I stepped forward—once, twice—stalking him as he continued to retreat. When his feet hit the water, the resultant splash made him pause, and at last I encircled him with my arms. "All I care about, Will Shakespeare, is you."

Would he have smiled? Would his arms have gone about me as well? Would he have agreed that nothing else mattered but the two of us? I cannot say.

For in the next instant, the world shimmied; the very air rippled like the waves upon the ocean at Will's back.

Then the ocean was gone. Will was gone.

And I was standing alone before the waterfall I had so recently wished to see.

Chapter Twenty

"Thought is free."
—*The Tempest* (Act III, scene 2)

The diamond stared at the falling water as if she had never seen such a thing before. But she recovered quickly, as hunters must do, glanced around, saw her sword, and retrieved it.

No wonder Shakespeare had killed the zombies, leaving Katherine to crouch in the trees and watch. When Ariel had transported the *chasseur,* she had forgotten to transport her weapon. She was lucky Katherine was not dead like the rest.

"Fool," Ariel muttered.

Her diamond crouched, blade at the ready, gaze flicking up then left and right. "Who goes there?" she demanded.

Ariel tilted her head, hovering just above the woman but invisible. Had she spoken out loud? Apparently.

"'Tis I," Ariel responded. She *had* brought the woman here to talk.

"Ariel?" The *chasseur* lowered the weapon, though she did not put it back down.

"Who else?"

"What mischief are you about? Where is Will? Bring him hence!"

"I do not take orders from you," Ariel said.

"You'd do better to take them from me than that lunatic you call *master*."

"You have seen him?" Ariel's very limbs stiffened; her neck did ache; her belly clenched and roiled.

"Aye."

"And he has seen you?" Worse and worse.

If Prospero knew a zombie hunter lurked upon the island, there was no telling what spell he might find in his book to thwart her. And if he discovered that Ariel had brought the woman hence, Ariel would never be free of him.

"He has not."

The strange tension flowed away, and the pain disappeared. "You are a very smart diamond."

"I am not a diamond," Katherine muttered, but there was no heat to her words.

As long as Prospero was unaware of Katherine's presence, or her calling, Ariel could relax and ask the questions swirling in her mind. Considering Katherine's behavior with Shakespeare, both on the island and before, according to the creature that had been—was still?—her husband, the *chasseur* might have answers. Ariel knew of no one else who could.

"What does it mean when they say 'touch me again'?"

Katherine, who had been drawing lines in the dirt with the tip of her sword, looked up and to the left of where Ariel hovered. "What type of they?"

Ariel considered. The husband was no longer completely a man, nor was he completely a wolf, but something in between.

However, Ariel desired the woman's response in regard to

the man, as men—and not bespelled half men—were what Katherine knew. Or at least this one, when he had yet been pure man.

"Men," Ariel answered.

The diamond's dark, well-formed eyebrows lifted. "There are many who have said this to you?"

"Nay." Ariel's cheeks felt afire. "But one."

"Ah," Katherine murmured, as if Ariel had said so much more than she had.

"Also," Ariel continued, "he said, 'No one has ever touched me like you did.'"

Katherine's lips curved. Was she remembering the same words being said to her by the same man and enjoying them all over again?

Ariel's belly flared, the fiery pain causing her hand to lift, her finger to point, her mouth to nearly spit a curse. She refrained, but only because she wanted the truth, and she would not get it from a two-headed goat.

"Did your husband say such to you?" The question came out sharper than Ariel intended, most likely because her belly still blazed.

"My husband never said much at all."

The woman spoke too quickly, and she stared at the ground. Ariel smelled a lie. She thought Katherine's husband *had* said much. Though perhaps not that.

"Did he press his lips to yours?"

"A kiss?"

"Is that what such an embrace is called?" The diamond nodded. "Then aye. Did he kiss you sweetly?"

"Never."

This admission—spoken firmly after the *chasseur* had

straightened her back and lifted her chin—reeked of truth and made the fire in Ariel's stomach fade.

"We did not marry for love," Katherine continued. "I will not mourn his death, as he did not mourn mine."

Interesting. Katherine thought her husband dead. Which made sense. The woman did not know of the confusion with the spell. And if truth be told, wasn't the man she'd married gone? A caliban had taken his place. However, Katherine's words brought up another question—one that same creature had posed.

"How could he mourn your death when you are not dead?"

Katherine glanced up again. "Can you not reveal yourself to me? It is unsettling to speak to the air. More so to have the air speak back."

"If I could do so, I would." Ariel floated downward, hovering just above the ground so the diamond would not get a pain in her neck. "My master ordered me subject to no sight but his and mine, invisible to every eyeball else."

"How is it, then, that Will sees you?"

"He is not human."

Katherine stiffened. "He told you this?"

"I saw."

The *chasseur*'s eyes did narrow. "What did you see?"

"Enough. How can you prefer a monster to a man?"

The diamond's lips tightened as her chin went up. "Sometimes a man is more of a monster than a monster could ever be."

"I do not understand."

"Pray you never do."

Ariel was tempted to press the issue, but she had too many others at hand. "You love this vampire. You kissed his face. You—"

"You watched us?"

"Why would I not?"

"It is impolite."

"If you did not want anyone to watch, then why did you do that which you wanted no one to see, where anyone could?"

"'Tis a *deserted* isle."

"Not really," Ariel remarked.

"Touché." Katherine lifted her sword, touched the flat to her forehead, then lowered it again. "Go on."

Ariel had to think a moment to remember where she had been. "You love the vampire," she repeated.

"I do."

"What is love?"

Katherine's mouth opened, then shut, then opened again, yet she said nothing.

"You do not know?" Ariel asked.

"It is hard to explain." Katherine paused, raising her free hand to keep Ariel from speaking. "This holy fire of Love, a dateless lively heat."

"What sayest thou?"

"Will's words. He writes of love better than anyone in the English language."

Mayhap love explained the fire in Ariel's belly, the heat in her limbs that had caused her to flee Caliban's words.

"Tell me more," Ariel demanded.

"Love hath chased sleep from my enthralled eyes and made them watchers of mine own heart's sorrow."

"Nay," Ariel murmured. She did not sleep—upon this isle few did unless compelled—and she felt no sorrow, only confusion.

And that incessant burning.

"There was another. So beautiful and so true. Hold." Katherine lifted her hand again. "I must think."

Ariel wanted to slap the woman with magic that would make everything Katherine knew fly from her lips. But Ariel had learned that such a spell set upon a human often made things tumble free that one did not wish to hear. So she waited, though waiting was not something she enjoyed.

"Love is not love which alters when it alteration finds, or bends with the remover to remove. O no! it is an ever-fixed mark, that looks on tempests and is never shaken."

"Tempests?" Ariel repeated, intrigued. If she controlled the tempest, could she not then control love?

Katherine continued as if Ariel had not spoken. "It is the star to every wand'ring bark, whose worth's unknown."

Caliban did bark. Did Katherine speak of that? Nay. The diamond did not know that her husband now possessed a snout.

If only Ariel could understand what on earth the woman was *saying*.

"What is love?" she asked again.

"Ethereal. Changing yet always the same. Consuming. Painful joy. Delicious heartache. Everything, yet nothing at all."

"You speak in riddles."

"It is the best I can do."

"How did you know 'twas love?"

Katherine sighed—the sound one of both longing and fulfillment. "I just did."

"I do not know, but yet . . ." Ariel considered. "I *feel*. It is most disconcerting."

"Ah," the diamond murmured. "Mayhap you lust."

"Be plain," Ariel ordered.

Katherine's lips did purse; her brow did crease. "My love has written of it thus. I have seen a medicine that's able to breathe life into a stone, quicken a rock, and make you dance canary."

"Canary?" Ariel asked.

"'Tis a court dance. Very lively," the diamond explained before continuing, "With spritely fire and motion, whose simple touch is powerful."

"Aye," Ariel whispered. "I was a stone until his simple touch made me dance." Or at least made her stomach do so.

Though he had not truly touched but rather sliced. What had the diamond said about joyful pain? The perfect words for all that roiled within her.

"Lust is nothing to sneeze at," Katherine remarked.

"Sneeze?" Ariel asked. 'Twas not something she did any more than sleep.

"Lust," Katherine continued, "some say passion, can be more overwhelming than love."

"Aye," Ariel agreed. "I believe it is so."

"And passion can deepen to love." Katherine's gaze searched for Ariel again, then she addressed the air several inches too high. "Who did you touch?"

"'Tis no matter."

"How did you touch him?"

"I patted him upon the head."

Katherine laughed. "Like a dog?"

He did resemble one. "I touched his face."

"Gently? While peering deeply into his eyes?"

"Aye." Ariel heard the sigh in her voice, which echoed the sigh the diamond had made when she'd spoken of falling in love.

Passion or love? Ariel did not know, and it appeared Katherine could not tell her. But there were still questions her diamond *could* answer.

"How came your husband to mourn your death when you are not yet dead?"

Katherine blinked at the sudden change of subject, but she responded. "I plotted a false death to be free of said husband."

"'Twas a treacherous thing to do."

"Mayhap." Katherine did not seem disturbed by it. "But then he was a treacherous husband."

Treacherous? That did not seem at all like the man-beast she knew.

"How so?" she asked.

"He wooed me with false words. Spoke of love, though he felt it not."

"Did you?"

"I believed I did at the time. When I discovered my husband loved my money and not my person, it hurt me. But it did not break me."

"Because you did not love him." Ariel's heart seemed to dance.

"Aye," Katherine agreed. "Once I knew Will . . ." She paused, considered, then continued, "For where thou art, there is the world itself . . . and where thou are not, desolation."

Yesterday Ariel would not have understood the words. Today she did. "Without Shakespeare—" she began.

"I would die."

"Thou *will* die," Ariel said. "And he will not."

Katherine cast a quick glance toward the air that sprouted Ariel's voice. "He can be killed."

"Not easily. Unlike you."

The *chasseur* twirled her sword against the ground, her lips quirked. "I am not as easily killed as you might think."

"What happens when you grow old, and he remains ever young?"

"I . . ." Katherine's smirk faded. "Do not know."

"You think he will love you when you are gray and wrinkled, when you can no longer leap and run and kill?"

"I do," Katherine said, but there was no strength behind it.

"There is a simple solution," Ariel said, wishing to help her diamond as her diamond had helped her.

"What?"

"You could become like him."

Chapter Twenty-one

"O brave monster! Lead the way."
—*The Tempest* (Act II, scene 2)

Reginald had bared his heart. He had never done so before. He was not sure why he did so now. Mayhap because he had never felt the way he felt when Ariel touched him. As if he would die if she never did so again.

Was this what his wife had experienced at Shakespeare's touch? If so, he began to understand why Katherine had behaved as she had. She would have been enraptured. As he was.

Despite Reginald's monstrous appearance, Ariel continued to treat him as a man. Despite his having sliced off her head and cut deeply her arm, she did not hate him. Of course, healing such injuries in a trice went a long way toward forgiving their cause.

His words—*No one has ever touched me like you did*—yet hung upon the misty air. Reginald waited for her response, still staring at the distant sea, afraid if he turned he would see the horror upon her face now that had never been there before.

After a long time passed, he murmured: "Ariel?"

Nothing answered but the breeze.

Reginald spun. And discovered himself alone on the mountaintop.

His shoulders slumped. He did not have to see Ariel's face. Her disappearance told him all he needed to know. She would not touch him again. No one would.

He'd hoped that the changes on the outside, which had sparked changes on his inside, would have also altered how others perceived him. No longer an ugly man but a beautiful beast, he felt different. He *was* different. But apparently no one had noticed but him.

Lifting his snout, Reginald howled his pain and fury to the dying sun then fell onto all fours and ran down the slope, putting behind him the place where he'd dared to dream.

Reginald raced through the jungle at a killing pace, the trees spinning backward, the brush clawing at his fur. He did not care. If he misstepped and ran headlong into a tree, he could break his neck. He wondered if he wanted to.

Reginald was still pondering that question when he did crash into something. Not a tree. 'Twas not so tall or hard. Nevertheless, he was thrown onto his back, where he stared at the darkening sky.

Slowly, he sat up, waiting for the pain, feeling none. Then he saw what he had hit.

"You!" he exclaimed.

Will Shakespeare sat likewise on the ground, a bit dazed as well. He rubbed at his chest, where the two of them must have bumped, lifted his gaze, and frowned. "Do I know you?" He tilted his head. "What *are* you?"

Reginald climbed onto two feet, towering over Shakespeare, who yet sat in the dirt. He quite liked it. The man—who was *not* a man—was too confident, too handsome, too smart, too talented.

Too everything Reginald was not. His dream shattered, fury raged.

"I am Caliban," he roared. "King of this jungle!"

Shakespeare also came to his feet. Unfortunately, he now towered over Reginald.

Filthy bung.

"Caliban," Shakespeare murmured. "Half man, half monster."

"How came you to know this?"

"The sorcerer tried to make me one as well."

Reginald's annoyance flared ever higher. *He* was Caliban. There could be none other.

"If Prospero wanted you to become half man, half beast, how is it that you still appear all man?" Reginald asked.

Thou misbegotten, hell-hated boar-pig.

Shakespeare looked away. "The spell did not work."

Because you are not a man, Reginald thought. But he said nothing. How would he explain such knowledge?

He did not have to. Shakespeare glanced at him, a considering expression upon his face. "I suspect it is because my humanity died centuries ago, when I did."

Reginald decided to play the dunce. According to his tutors, he was very good at it.

"How can you say you have died, yet here you stand before me?"

"I am undead," Shakespeare said, his face a picture of sadness, yet he still appeared more handsome than most men did whilst happy.

And alive.

Thou artless fat-kidneyed death-token.

Shakespeare cast him a quick glance. "What did thou sayest?"

"What is undead?"

"Vampire," Shakespeare said simply.

"Thou sustainest thyself on the livers of small children?"

The vampire's mouth tightened. "Hardly. I partake of blood now and again. Never from children."

Reginald did not have to pretend his disgust. Blood sickened him.

"Dost thou fly through the night on a broomstick?"

"That would be a witch."

Reginald clapped his paws. "A great black bat."

"I cannot fly."

Reginald resisted the urge to smirk. Mayhap the impertinent rump-fed measle could *not* do everything. "Pity."

"Yes," Shakespeare agreed.

"Dost thou dance on the bones of nuns and piss upon holy ground?"

Shakespeare's eyes narrowed. "I do not piss at all."

"How can that be?"

"How can *I* be?" Shakespeare returned.

Good point.

"And the nuns?" Reginald could not resist asking.

"No." Shakespeare's voice was clipped.

Reginald tried to grin at the vampire's annoyance, and his overly large tongue lolled from his snout. His attempt at manly chuckles rolled free instead as a series of barks.

"What a horrible sound," Shakespeare said. "For the first time in many a year I applaud my lack of humanity. I have no desire to bark."

Reginald's good cheer died. He searched for a way to get it back.

"You would rather lie in a coffin and fear the daylight?"

Shakespeare sighed. "Let me tell you true. Only the morning sun can harm me, and I may lie anywhere that I like. I often do."

A growl rumbled in Reginald's chest when he considered where the bastard had been lying of late.

Shakespeare cast him a glance then continued. "Garlic is useless, as is a crucifix. I will live long and prosper."

He paused as if someone had called his name then looked up. "Hmm," he murmured. "A trek to the stars. A strange, pointy-eared, overly logical man. 'Twould be interesting."

"Are you mad?" Reginald asked.

Shakespeare blinked then lowered his gaze. "Merely a writer."

"Some might say they are one and the same."

The bard's lips curved. "Some might."

"You truly believe you will never die."

"I never said 'never.' But I will surely outlive you."

The growl now pushed at Reginald's throat. "Think you so?"

The vampire shrugged. "I do not age. When I first became undead, centuries upon centuries ago, I appeared exactly as I do now."

Handsome and young forever. The pottle-deep popinjay. How did some men have all the luck?

"Have you seen a woman?" Shakespeare asked. "Tall and trim. Dark of hair and eye."

"I have not," Reginald lied. "Who is she?"

"My life."

"You are dead," Reginald pointed out, earning another glowering glance from the bard.

"Hence my need for life."

"She is not like you?"

"She walks in sunshine; I live in shadow. She is breath; I am death."

Reginald saw a way to tarnish Shakespeare's golden un-life and took it.

"She lives but one life," Reginald said, "while you live many."

"The only life worth living is the one I am living with her."

"How sad it will not last."

The dreamy expression upon Shakespeare's face faded. "What say you?"

"She will age," Reginald continued, hearing in his voice the echo of the serpent in Eve's garden and liking it.

"Aye." The man's high, perfect brow creased.

"She will die," Reginald whispered. "You will watch."

"Aye." The poet's gaze became distant again, even as his face once more reflected a deep sadness.

"It would be best to . . ." Reginald trailed off, waiting for Shakespeare's attention to return. He wanted the vampire to hear this—to hear and consider, to agonize and then to pine.

It took a while, but eventually the bard's eyes flicked to Reginald's, their focus no longer removed. "I beg thy pardon. It would be best to . . . ?"

"Set her free," Reginald finished. "'Twould avoid a lot of pain later on." Or, mayhap, cause a lot of pain now, which Reginald could watch.

"But—" Shakespeare began.

"You cannot give her a normal life."

"She does not want one."

"Women say many things in the gloss of new love." Reginald had no idea what women in love said, having never been near one, but it must be true, as Shakespeare nodded slowly.

"And what of children?" Reginald asked.

The vampire paused mid-nod. "What of them?"

"How can you have children if their livers call to your hunger?"

"I do *not* eat the livers of children," Shakespeare said, teeth grinding together so loudly he might have been chewing upon rocks. "However . . ."

"Yes?"

"I cannot give her children. I am . . ." He waved vaguely in the area of his codpiece. "Dead."

"A shame." Reginald pursed his lips. "Women need a live rod."

"I did not say I could not—" Shakespeare broke off again, exasperated. "I can satisfy a woman; I cannot give anyone a child."

The image of Shakespeare satisfying Reginald's *wife* as Reginald had never been able to caused a resurgence of his unreasoning fury. He pushed that image aside and returned to his reptilian task.

"A shame," he repeated. "Women like children."

"Not Kate." Shakespeare's lips pursed. "Well, she likes them well enough, but she does not want any of her own."

"There is a difference between not wanting and never, ever being able to have."

Reginald's barb apparently hit home, because Shakespeare's face clouded, and he wandered off in the direction he'd come without so much as a halfhearted farewell.

If Reginald yet possessed feet, he might have danced. He would wager that soon the perfectly brilliant, handsome

Shakespeare would inform the love of his lives that he had no further interest in her at all.

Reginald laughed, pausing when the hoarse bark made his overly sensitive ears ache. Instead he fell onto all fours and loped into the jungle, tongue trailing, spittle flying—the closest thing he could manage to a grin.

His work here was done.

Chapter Twenty-two

"There's nothing ill can dwell in such a temple."

—*The Tempest* (Act I, scene 2)

"Become like him?" I echoed.

"Aye," Ariel said. "If you were not so easy to kill, think how many more zombies you could destroy. Not just here and now, but everywhere and for a long, long time."

I did think, and I liked what came to mind. Being able to perform my duties without the concern that a *tibonage* might eliminate me first was tremendously appealing. I did not worry about my own end whilst in battle—I could not and fight with any sort of courage—but there were nights when sleep eluded me, my mind swamped with imagined horrors, and nights where I *did* sleep but my dreams were filled with images of zombies come to devour me.

"You would not need to fear growing old," Ariel continued.

"I have never feared that." Because I had known the odds I *would* were highly unlikely.

But now, with Will at my side, protecting me, the chances of dying young had slimmed, thereby increasing the likelihood that I would grow old, while Will . . .

Would not.

"What would it be like for him to watch you wither and die?" I flinched. "You could avoid causing him such pain. You could be together for always. If I were you, I'd become a vampire today."

I had never entertained the idea. Will's identity as a necro-vampire had been revealed to me only a short time ago. Between saving the queen, killing the one who would have killed her and all the minions he had raised, faking my own death, going down with the ship, and being stranded on Zombie Island, I had not had the opportunity to entertain much.

The sudden absence of the waterfall's crash had me spinning in that direction, only to discover I was again on the beach. If I did not now have my sword in hand, I would have believed I imagined the entire interlude.

"There you are." Will's voice sounded from behind me.

I turned from the ocean as he emerged from the trees. "Where were you?"

"Searching for you." He seemed troubled, but considering I'd disappeared into thin air, that was understandable.

"Ariel wanted to speak with me," I said.

"Ah."

Will hovered at the edge of the jungle, gaze unfocused. That he did not ask me what the sprite had wanted only made me believe his current distraction was more about the words, characters, places, and plots that often tumbled through his head rather than my disappearance.

As we were both still filthy with zombie ash, I set my sword far away from the waves then led Will to the water.

This time when I undressed him, then myself, he did not protest. He remained immobile while I washed him, his gaze on the sun as it died. My fingers scrubbed the ash from his hair, the dirt from his neck, the blood from his face. As my touch became closer to caress than cleanse, he awakened, stirring below the surface.

"Kate," he began, and stepped back.

"Will," I returned, and followed.

The water now reached his waist. The muscles of his stomach rippled like the sea. I licked my lips, tasting salt and him.

His gaze followed the movement of my tongue. He tried to look away but couldn't. "We should—"

I twined my arms about his neck, pressing my body the length of his. "Aye, we should."

Ariel's words of death and loss, while making me consider for the first time a solution, had also reminded me that life was short at least mine—and I should love Will at every opportunity.

"We must search for zombies, survivors. Something."

"'Tis an island. If there are any, they will be there when we are through."

"But we just—"

I put my fingers to his lips. "Aye, we just. Which only makes me want to again."

"I don't think I can."

The pulse of him against my belly proved the lie. But I shrugged and turned about, making sure to brush my hip against him as I did. "Then help me." I shook the tumbling dark tresses, no doubt sending zombie ash into his face. "I need to wash them out."

"You want me to . . ."

"Wash those men right out of my hair."

He stilled, and I lifted my gaze, fearing an army of the

dead had emerged from the trees. But the beach remained empty.

I glanced over my shoulder; Will had gone away again in his mind.

"Another island," he murmured. "Where it is always warm. Soldiers. Nay, seamen. A nurse who loves one man—"

I stiffened. "Nurse?"

I had been spied upon by Reginald's childhood nurse and had no stomach for the lot of them any longer. I would not have one made a heroine through Will's genius. In truth, I would prefer he make every nurse who appeared in his plays a fool.

"Not that kind," he said. "But one who heals the sick. She is strange, this nurse. She loves a man, but cannot accept his children. She sings of her troubles—" He snapped his fingers. "They all do! The songs move forth the plot."

I lifted a brow. I had always been enamored of the theater and knew quite a bit about it. This had allowed me to perform at the Rose under the guise of Clayton, boy actor. It had also set the stage for Will and me to fall in love. We'd worked together both to hunt zombies and to create, practice, and present his plays. Performing had been as wonderful as I'd always dreamed it would be.

"Interesting," I murmured. "I don't believe such has been done before."

Music was often included in plays, but more as a lighter section to relieve the darkness of a tragedy. Mayhap an amusement during a comedy. Or there might be a performance for a king during a history play—a musicale within the larger structure. But to have the music be part of the play itself? 'Twas—

"Genius," I said.

Will's lips curved. "The nurse sings as she washes her hair of how she will—"

"Wash that man right out." I laughed. So clever. "Do so for me now, Will." He set his hands on my head, and I covered them with my own. "But know that I will never want to wash you away."

"Never is a very long time."

At the sadness in his voice, I began, again, to turn, thinking I would tell him what Ariel had said, the solution she had put forth. But Will held me in place, and I found that I could not speak of it without looking him in the eye. Within seconds, I no longer recalled what I'd been about to say.

Will washed those men—or those who had once been men— right out of my hair, then he turned his attention to the rest of me.

By the time the moon shone across the gently rolling waves, he was my Will again. Stroking me, kissing me, loving me as only he could—with hands and lips and exquisite words.

"Dost thou love me?" His fingertips followed the lap of the waves along the swell of my breasts.

I opened my mouth, and he pressed those fingertips to it. "I know thou wilt say 'Aye,' and I will take thy word."

My mouth curved against his skin, and I let my tongue snake out. He tasted of the night, the sea, and the moon—of Will, my one true love.

"Lady," he whispered, dropping his hand, "by yonder blessed moon I swear—"

"Oh, swear not by the moon," I interrupted. "The inconstant moon, that monthly changes in her circled orb. Lest that thy love prove likewise variable."

I adored bantering words, lines that might be used upon

the stage later or found in sonnets meant secretly for me. 'Twas what he did, what *we* did, and it both aroused and humbled me.

His head tilted. "Comparing the moon's waxing and waning to the uncertainty of newfound love. I like it."

"I like you."

He smiled. "If not the moon, then what shall I swear by?"

"Do not swear at all. Or if thou wilt, swear by thy gracious self." I set my palm upon his cheek and stared into his endless eyes. "Which is the god of my idolatry."

"Kate." His smile became a frown. "I pray you speak lines of a play and not your truth."

"You *are* the god of my idolatry." I slid my fingers through his tangled, wet hair, running my thumb then my tongue along his earring as I whispered: "I worship you. Body, mind, and soul."

"Kate, I have no—" he began, but I plunged on.

"Make me like you, Will." I leaned back, the sheen of the moon sliding across my neck as I offered myself to him forever. "Turn me now."

Chapter Twenty-three

"What seest thou else
In the dark backward and abysm of time?"

—*The Tempest* (Act I, scene 2)

Horrified, Will dropped her.

Thankfully they were in the water, and Kate did not fall far or hard. She did slap against the surface of the waves, sink beneath, emerge choking.

And furious.

"Wh—?" Cough.

"Wha—?" Spit.

"Ass!" she managed at last.

Will spread his hands. "I am sorry."

He wasn't. She'd needed a good dunk if only to get her mind right.

"I tell you I worship you. That I want to be like you. I offer you my life. And you drop me beneath the sea?"

She shoved him in the chest. Will stepped back, just to make her happy. She couldn't move him if she chose to throw her whole body at his person.

"Kate, you are blinded by love."

Love looks not with the eyes, but with the mind, and therefore is wing'd Cupid painted blind.

"Shh," he muttered. 'Twas beautiful, but not *now*!

"Do not shush me."

Her eyes narrowed; her fingers curved into fists. Will was lucky she had left her sword upon the beach when she had drawn him into the water.

"And I am not blind, Will Shakespeare. In truth, my eyes now clearly see."

"You are not seeing, or thinking, clearly if you believe I will make you a monster." Her fingers unfurled even as his clenched. "Like me."

"You are not a monster."

"I was, and I could easily be so again."

He *had* been so only a few short days ago. Thankfully Kate had been unconscious at the time—thanks to him—and had not seen the destruction he had wrought in order to save both her and his queen. He'd had no choice, but what he had done had not been pretty.

Or human.

Will could no longer stand here in the moon-silver water, with her so near and them so naked. He headed for the beach and the safety of his clothes. "I would not have you dead, Kate."

She followed. "Undead and dead are not the same."

Will began to dress. "Undead arises from dead. I would have to kill you, and that I cannot do."

He shook the sand out of his doublet with more force than was necessary. Granules flew everywhere, some stuck to Kate's still damp face. She spit a few off her tongue, casting him a narrow glare before picking up her shift then flicking it and tossing sand into his face as well. "You did kill me, or have you forgotten our plot?"

Will left the sand where it had stuck. He had bigger problems than sand. "You were not truly dead. The potion only made you appear so."

"And I would not be *truly* dead if you made me like you."

"Do not ask this of me, Kate." He stared at his bare, sand-encrusted feet and not at her. "Do not."

"But . . ." Her voice was a mere wisp in the night. "Why?"

"There are things in life you cannot have in undeath."

"Nothing that matters."

He sighed. She was so damned young.

"You do not realize until it is gone how much you miss what you have lost."

"Like what?"

"The dawn."

"I care not for the dawn."

"When you have not seen a sunrise for a few centuries, you will care." He lifted his head and stared at the bright, silver, slightly lopsided moon. 'Twas beautiful but so cold. Like him. "You will miss it like you miss your family, your home, your friends."

"You are my family, my home, and my friend." She set her hand on his arm, and he lowered his gaze from the moon to her. "The dawn is a small thing to give up, Will, if I could always and forever have you."

"You *will* always have me."

"I will die and you will not. I will grow old, if I am lucky and the *tibonage* do not feast upon my brains, and you will always be like . . ." She waved her hand to indicate his sand-strewn person. "This."

Will scowled. "You have talked with Caliban."

"Who?"

"The half-man, half-wolf creature that runs about upon this isle."

"There's another running about on the isle? And he is—" She tilted her head. "What?"

"The beast was created by Prospero. He tried to make me one as well, remember? Half man, half monster. Behold! But since I was not human, the spell did not work."

Kate nodded then glanced toward the jungle. "I have not seen this creature, or spoken with him."

"Then where did you get such a foolish idea?"

"It is not foolish!" Her eyes, filled with both anger and despair, met his. "'Twill solve all our problems."

"No, sweet Kate, 'twill only give us more of them." He tossed a hand in the direction of the clearing where he had killed so many. "You saw what I did but a few hours past."

Confusion flickered amid the despair. "I do not know what you mean."

"I tore the heads off people with my bare hands, if not my teeth. Were you not horrified? Disgusted? Frightened?"

Her confusion deepened. "They were not people any longer, Will."

"And if I make you like me, you will not be people any longer either."

She began to laugh, but at his tortured expression quickly stopped. "Is that what you truly believe? That you are not human?"

"I am not. The very curse Prospero attempted to put upon me proved it. To become half man, half beast, I first had to be a man. I am not."

"You have played the man with me many times and very well."

"I died, Kate. I rose again as something not of this earth. I walk the night. I drink blood."

She shrugged. "No one is perfect."

"I will not do that to you."

"You would have me die?"

"No." He crossed the short distance between them and touched her face. "I would have you *live*."

Chapter Twenty-four

"Now would I give a thousand furlongs
of sea for an acre of barren ground."

—*The Tempest* (Act I, scene 1)

"Ariel! Come hither, spirit, and make haste."

Ariel, who had been in the midst of her conversation with the diamond, glanced up at Prospero's distant call. Katherine, deep in thought, did not seem to hear.

A single wave sent the woman back where Ariel had found her. An instant later, the fairy materialized from the air in front of her master. "Aye, sire. Thou didst bellow?"

"Where are my zombies? I have traversed this isle from side to side." He indicated a path from east to west. "And again." He pointed north to south. "I found nothing but blood and ashes and trees."

At least he had not found her diamond. Ariel hated to think what he might do if he discovered his sprite had brought a zombie hunter to kill his zombie army before he could make use of it.

"Mayhap they took refuge from the sun in a cool, dark cave," she suggested.

Prospero frowned. "They do not have the brains to step free of the sun on their own. Did you lead them there?"

Ariel opened her mouth, planning to tell him that she had, that even now his zombie army reclined safe and sound nearby—the more zombies the man thought he had, the fewer he would order her to raise—and found she could not. She might be able to talk around the truth, but she could not knowingly tell an untruth.

At least to him.

"I did not," she said.

Her master's smug expression told her he had known that already. Mayhap the question had been a test.

"Considering the amount of ash I found, someone killed them." His bushy brows lowered. "Know you anything of this?"

Even as she shook her head, three words sprung out. " 'Twas the vampire."

And the *chasseur*. And the caliban.

Ariel managed to keep the latter two answers locked within. Apparently if she told a half-truth, she could avoid telling the whole truth.

"Vampire, you say?" Prospero stroked his chin. "That dost explain a few things." His gaze skewered Ariel. "How did this happen?"

"I did as you bade me," Ariel blurted. "I drowned all men upon the ships. But he was not a man. He could not drown. He does not breathe." She lowered her head. "It was not my fault."

Silence settled between them, and Ariel waited for the shouting to begin. Her master would never free her now, and he did not even know all that she had done.

"Of course it was not your fault."

Ariel looked up. Prospero smiled, opening his arms wide as

if he would hug her. She stayed where she was, out of hugging distance. The very idea of an embrace made her silver skin crawl, although the concept of a hug from another—Caliban, for instance—made her skin ripple in an entirely different way.

Prospero lowered his hands, one still clutching his cursed book, to his sides. "Who would guess that a vampire would be on a sailing ship? 'Tis an accident most provident."

"Provident?" Ariel echoed.

"If he is what I think he is—and why would he not be? 'Tis too great a twist of fate that one such as he would arrive here and not be useful—then this is further proof that my claim is just, and my methods . . ." His smile deepened. "Are the methods of a king."

Ariel thought his methods were those of a madman, but she would do well to keep that thought to herself. He had not asked her opinion, and giving it would not make him any less mad, mayhap only more so.

"A ship approaches." Ariel followed the tilt of her master's head and saw that one did, indeed, approach. "Sink it. More will follow."

He strode off without waiting to see if she complied with his order. She always did; she had little choice.

As he disappeared into the jungle, his voice drifted to her on the steadily increasing wind.

"Stand fast, good Fate," he murmured. "Make the rope of his destiny our cable. I am in need of help, and help the gods did provide."

Chapter Twenty-five

"If it should thunder as it did before,
I know not where to hide my head."

—*The Tempest* (Act II, scene 2)

Reginald had been running through the jungle, lighter of feet and of heart as a caliban than he had ever been as a man. Then distant thunder made him stop, his claws rowing furrows in the dirt, as the sudden electricity on the air made his ruff lift.

He sniffed, caught the scent of the sea, and shifted in that direction. If there was another tempest afoot, he wanted to know of it.

However, as Reginald neared the shore, raised voices drifted on the wind. Shakespeare and Reginald's own wife. They were arguing.

He crouched low, belly skimming the ground, and inched forward until he could see as well as hear.

Shakespeare had been cupping Katherine's face, staring into her eyes, but she shoved him in his well-muscled chest and spun away.

"I will not live long like this," she shouted.

"If I make you like me," Shakespeare retorted, "you will no longer *live* at all."

Reginald's insidious words were causing more trouble than he could have hoped. Shakespeare appeared ready to shake his dear love until her teeth rattled free of her head. Katherine seemed eager to kick her new toy in the balls. Instead, she threw up her hands. "How can you not see the truth of this?"

"Because I have seen a truth you have not, and I pray you never do."

Reginald wondered: If a vampire dared to pray, would he burst into flames? Mayhap he would be struck by lightning?

Thunder rumbled again, closer now, and the clouds did roil. Reginald wiggled his rump, and the greenery surrounding him shook. He dug his claws into the dirt and ordered himself to be still.

"What truth?" Katherine asked, words clipped.

"The truth of what happens when a human is changed."

"They live instead of die. They do not age; they do not sicken. And those who wish to kill them have a very, very hard time."

Shakespeare sighed, and when he spoke the words were so quiet Reginald would not have been able to hear if he had not been changed himself.

"The bloodlust is all that lives in a body become undead. At first we are out of control, there is never enough. The hunger is all that there is. With that need pounding in the brain, a newly made vampire will kill. He cannot help himself. All he knows is that he needs more."

He drew in a breath, even though he no longer needed to. 'Twas just for show. Shakespeare was forever an actor upon life's stage.

"And a vampire can get more," he continued. "'Tis not difficult. The world is our banquet."

"You told me," Katherine began, then took a breath of her own. However, hers shook, and she paused, hands clenching, face canted downward as she attempted to rein in her emotions. "You told me that as time passes the lust can be controlled. *You* rarely drink blood."

"I am old. It took me centuries to become strong enough to resist the sweet allure." His face softened; he lifted his hand as if he would touch her, then let it fall away before ever getting close. "And still, when I drank from you, I was tempted back to the way I had been."

The gleeking toad-spotted scut had drunk from her? Disgusting!

"You had no choice, Will. You needed strength to save the queen, strength to kill the monster that would have killed her. That would have killed us."

"Aye," he agreed. "But . . ." He paused, looking away. "I enjoyed it."

She blinked, obviously shocked, but quickly regained her composure "Y-you say that to frighten me. You curbed your need for blood long ago. You became again who you were before you died."

"We never become again exactly who we were, sweet Kate, because dead can never again be alive."

"I do not understand your obsession with breathing," she snapped. "You are the most wonderful of men—brilliant, passionate yet gentle, brave, and true. I will love you for the rest of my life." Katherine's voice lowered to just above a whisper. "I could love you for the rest of *your* life if you would but let me."

Shakespeare remained silent for several moments, staring at the ground and not at her. "I have killed people, Kate. So many I do not even recall their names."

"You need not worry. They will continue to stop by night and day to remind you."

Reginald tilted his head. Not only was the bard a vampire, but he saw ghosts.

And people thought Reginald a freak.

"If their constant presence, their never-ending whispers, were not recompense enough," Katherine continued, "you write their stories so they will never be forgotten."

"'Tis *not* enough," Shakespeare said. "But it is a small comfort. One you would never have, since I was born with my affinity for the dead. You would kill, Kate, but never be able to atone."

"I could keep a list," she snapped.

"Of course." Shakespeare swept a deep, sarcastic bow. "Pardon me, sir, before I kill you may I know your name? Give me leave to write it down. Do not move. I will drink from your veins until you expire, by the by."

Katherine's eyes narrowed. "It would not be like that."

"No. Because in the throes of the bloodlust you would not care whom you killed or how many. You would not have the control to write down a name, let alone ask it of them in the first place."

"You would be there. You would help me."

"Kate, there is no help for that."

Silence settled between them, broken only by the sound of Katherine's harsh breath.

"Once you become again as you are now," Shakespeare continued, "or at least as close as you could get, I do not believe you would ever forgive me, or yourself, for what you had done."

Katherine at last appeared uncomfortable, and Shakespeare pressed the advantage. "You would have killed. Ripped out people's throats, drunk of their blood, laughed as they died."

"Nay," she whispered. "I would not. *You* did not."

"You are wrong." His voice and face were as stark as the slate gray shift of the sky.

"You are not like that, Will." The words were stronger, yet not strong enough. Katherine hoped she was right, but she wasn't certain.

Reginald wasn't certain either. He thought Shakespeare could easily have been as vicious and violent as he professed. After being on the receiving end of the man's anger himself, Reginald thought Shakespeare might still be. Although Reginald was beginning to understand the reason behind that violence.

Reginald had struck his wife. At the time, he'd believed he had cause. Now . . .

Reginald shifted again, this time with unease at his memories.

He had pretended at love. He had not understood until coming here, becoming this, that to do so was the greatest betrayal of all. He still did not appreciate Katherine's disloyalty with Shakespeare, but he was beginning to see how it had come about. Love made fools of everyone.

And as for Shakespeare's behavior . . . The horror Reginald had experienced after accidentally slicing Ariel's throat—even her arm—made him think that the sight of Katherine being struck had tossed Shakespeare over the edge.

The idea of anyone striking Ariel, for any reason, caused Reginald to want to tear out throats himself. Shakespeare had merely rapped Reginald's head against the wall until it ached. In truth, the vampire had shown tremendous restraint. Reginald was not sure he could control his own beast any better.

"I am not like that now," Shakespeare agreed, then clarified. "Not quite. But if you had seen me then, Kate, you would have been first in line to kill me."

Katherine did not answer. Most likely because she knew that Shakespeare was right.

According to Ariel, Reginald's wife was a zombie hunter. She killed monsters every night. So why, then, had she not killed Shakespeare the first time he revealed he had fangs?

"We cannot go on like this, Will."

"Why not?"

"Time passes, things change."

"I don't," he said.

"Exactly," she muttered, and walked away.

There were a hundred other bushes, ten other trees, a dozen different directions, yet she came straight toward Reginald. Had she seen him there after all?

He caught his breath, ducked his head, crept into the foliage, and hugged the ground from tail to snout. Katherine stomped past, so close the whisper of the fronds she displaced stirred the ends of his fur. But she did not stop. She did not shout: *Hie! A beast!* She did not stick him in the gut with her sword.

An instant later, the sounds of her passing faded. Reginald risked a peek above the greenery that hid him, but William Shakespeare had disappeared.

He nearly snuck out of his hiding place, but his new superior ears picked up the tramp of approaching footsteps despite the increasing wail of the wind, and Reginald remained exactly where he was.

Prospero appeared on the beach, staring out at the now white froth of the waves. On the horizon, the steadily heightening swells tossed several ships hither and yon. His long striped hair whipped straight away from his head, and his tattered robes ruffled, revealing old man parts better left unrevealed.

"Spirits," he murmured, "which by mine art I have from their confines call'd to enact my present fancies."

The old bastard was at it once more! The storm would wreck the vessels, releasing the living into the water, where they would soon become the dead. Prospero would raise them, and once again . . .

"Zombie Island," Reginald murmured.

His flanks wiggled as excitement flowed through him. He had enjoyed killing zombies. Probably the only thing he had in common with his wife. And here he'd thought they would never have anything in common at all.

A sharp laugh escaped—the barking hack drawing Prospero's attention. "How now! Who goes there?"

If Reginald could have stopped wiggling, he might have been able to keep his presence undetected despite the unfortunate bark, but he couldn't. The fronds directly above him shook even more violently from his excitement than all the others shook from the wind.

Prospero came closer and saw him. "I shall laugh myself to death at this puppy-headed monster. A most scurvy monster! Come out!"

Reginald would have preferred to stay right where he was. Puppy-headed? Scurvy? Indeed!

However, now that Prospero had found him, he doubted he would have a moment's peace. Considering what the old man had done to him already, Reginald decided not to test what the sorcerer might yet do if he disobeyed.

Reginald crept from his hiding place. He didn't even need to shake the leaves and needles from his fur. The whip of the wind did it for him; the discarded greenery rolled across Prospero's bare feet and away.

"Why didst thou conceal thyself?" The old man cast a narrow-eyed, suspicious glare at Reginald. "Hast thou done something for which thou shouldst be punished?"

If Prospero discovered Reginald had killed his precious zombies—

"The vampire did it," he blurted.

Prospero lifted his head. His eyes reflected not surprise—he must have heard about the vampire already—but rather a cool, reptilian interest. "Hast thou seen this vampire?"

"Aye. He was here but a few moments past. He and his lady love argued and—"

Prospero raised one long, crooked finger, and Reginald immediately fell silent. "What lady love?"

"Her name is Katherine." Reginald pursed his lips before both his own name and hers escaped.

"She drowned all *men* upon the ships." Prospero snapped his fingers. "Tricksy spirit. She has bested me with words."

Reginald saw his mistake. He never should have mentioned his wife at all. Now he had gotten Ariel into trouble. Eager to distract the sorcerer lest he practice mischief upon her, Reginald blurted the first thing that came to mind. "The vampire sees ghosts."

Prospero's thin lips curved. "I had thought that he might."

Reginald's mouth fell open, and his too-long tongue fell out. It took him a moment to reel it back in so he could ask: "How came you to think this?"

Prospero indicated the ancient tome he seemed to carry everywhere. "There is so much more in these pages than spells. Legends, answers, even questions abide within."

Reginald eyed the book. "Where did you get that?"

"I was told it belonged to my mother."

"And who was your mother?"

"A witch. And one so strong that could control the moon, make flows and ebbs."

Reginald was not surprised. How else would Prospero have become a sorcerer unless a witch had birthed him?

Had the witch who birthed Prospero been the same witch who had confined Ariel to the tree? Most likely. How many witches were there?

Strangely, he was not so afraid of witches anymore. As he was now, he did not have to be.

"Came she with you here?" Reginald asked.

"Nay. She never knew I existed."

Reginald tilted his puppy head. "How could she have birthed you and not known that you drew breath?"

"She was told I had died. I was kept hidden, a secret, eventually banished to this isle. A usurper sits upon my throne. I will have it back."

Not if Ariel had anything to say about it, but Reginald kept that thought to himself.

"I must find the vampire," Prospero said.

"That way." Reginald shot out a claw, narrowly missing Prospero's throat. The old man gave him a look that would have boiled brown from bark, but his gaze then softened.

"Worry not," he murmured. "What thou hast told me is helpful. I will not punish the sprite for her insolence, as it has given me the means to the end I didst desire."

Reginald's chest, which had been so tight he was having difficulty breathing without panting, relaxed.

"But tell her not that I have learned of her treachery." The old man smiled, but the expression held little pleasantry. "Unless you would like her to know how I learned of it?"

Reginald could do nothing but shake his head so frantically his ears slapped him in the eyes.

Prospero tapped his chin. "They were arguing, you say?"

"Aye."

"About what?"

Reginald waited for the rush of pride at how he had caused his false wife and her fanged lover to dance like puppets upon his string with very little effort at all. Instead, he was a little . . . ashamed.

Prospero snapped his fingers in front of Reginald's nose. "The argument?"

"She will die, and he will not," Reginald said. "She will age as he stays forever young."

"And?"

How could the man be so dense?

"She wants the vampire to make her one too."

Prospero's brows lifted. "He refused?"

"Aye."

"Why?"

"He would not have her become a murderous fiend upon her change. He would not sentence her to drink blood throughout eternity. He did not want her to become a monster. Like him."

"'Twould seem to me that he is far from a monster to think of her welfare above his own."

"What welfare?" Reginald asked. "His life is nigh on to perfect." Except for the blood drinking and the loss of the morning sun. But minor inconveniences all in all.

"He is not alive," Prospero said. "And while he may walk

the earth forever, he will do so alone for most of it." The fellow swept his hand out to indicate the isle, around which new storm clouds blossomed like an ebony rose. "I have been alone. I do not recommend it."

"Their plight is sad," Reginald agreed, and strangely, he *felt* sad. "It is unfortunate he cannot be made like her."

"Hmm," the old man murmured, brow furrowed, lips bunched into a pucker. "Hmm."

Then he threw back his head and cackled madly to the gathering storm before he patted Reginald upon the head and strode purposefully into the advancing fog.

Chapter Twenty-six

"He that dies pays all debts."
—*The Tempest* (Act III, scene 2)

Will Shakespeare would be the death of me!

I stomped through the jungle as storm clouds gathered overhead and tendrils of mist wound about my ankles.

"In one way or another," I muttered.

Either he would kill me then lift me again as I desired, or the broken heart caused by his denial would send me to my grave.

Better that than zombies.

I stopped walking so fast my head went light and dizzy. What if zombies killed me? Would Will deign to raise me then?

I put my hand over my mouth. What a horrible, frightening, *wonderful* idea.

Could I do it? I did not know.

I lifted my gaze to the turbulent sky. The new crop of zombies would not arrive before morn. Until then, I must avoid Will. He would take one look into my eyes and know I was not myself. He had such insight into human nature, mayhap he would decipher what I was about. Then, though he had sworn never again to use his vampire powers to "push" me, he would.

If only to make sure I did not throw myself into the gaping jaws of undeath.

Now, where to hide?

My gaze went to the mountain, where I could just make out the openings to several caves. I hurried in that direction. Long before I reached my destination I was soaked, the once white material of my shift gone transparent.

Rain cascaded down my face; my hair covered my eyes. Before I could reach up to swipe all away, I slammed into something less solid than a tree but more so than a bush.

I flew backward, landing hard on my backside. But I held on to my sword. I'd been tossed many times before and knew better than to let my weapon be tossed too.

The non-tree, non-bush, said: "Oomph."

I scraped my face clear of hair and rain then tightened my fingers around my sword as a strange creature arose.

Dirty blond fur covered the body of a man, but the hands, head, and feet were doglike. Although no dog I'd ever encountered possessed such beastly claws and teeth.

Then I remembered Will's words about the half man, half monster created by Prospero.

"Caliban," I murmured.

"How did you know?" His eyes, clear blue, were fixed upon me, and I experienced a shiver of recognition—most likely because of their all-too-human expression of curiosity and concern.

"I . . . um . . . heard the sorcerer attempt to cast the same spell upon another man."

The caliban snorted. Then, observing my frown, he sneezed, lifting his paw to his snout and nearly spearing himself in the eye with one claw.

"Attempt, you say?" His voice was both man and beast; rough, rumbling, it trilled across my damp, chilled skin like a feather.

The rain and wind increased, becoming a torrent. The creature cringed, obviously distressed. "Let us go where the storm cannot harm us," I said.

"Us?" he repeated, but he trotted at my side like a graceful hound as I led him to the dark oval of a cave. We stepped inside just as the sky opened and poured forth lightning.

Books covered every raised surface. Ragged clothes hung upon a rope. A pallet contained tousled bedding, and a banked fire glowed orange at the center. I moved forward and stoked it to life. "Someone has been living here."

"Prospero," the caliban said, and at my glance shrugged. "Who else?"

"Who else indeed?" I sat on a mat woven of grass. "I am Kate, by the by."

"Caliban," the creature returned. "But this you know."

"What was your name before . . ." I waved vaguely in the direction of his snout.

He looked away. "No matter."

I would have thought it mattered quite a lot, but then I had not been turned into a beast. Although . . .

I wanted to be.

"Why does it not matter?" I asked.

He had sat upon his haunches, gaze focused on the rain pouring down the mountainside and off the edge of the entrance like a sluice.

"Who I was before is gone," he said slowly, as if he were just realizing this himself.

"There is nothing of the former you left?"

"I have embraced this me. I am stronger, faster, better. No

one dares cross me." He lifted one paw and waggled his claws even as the firelight flashed off his equally sharp teeth. "I am Caliban, lord of this isle."

Caliban appeared as delusional as Prospero. However, considering the teeth and the claws, I decided to let him think whatever he wished.

"You would live here forever? Forsaking all that you know, all whom you loved?"

His tongue lolled out as he considered my questions. Before he could answer, he had to slurp it back in. Spittle fell into the fire and sizzled.

Oh, yes, he was definitely *better*.

"I have never loved."

"I am sorry to hear it."

He shifted his flanks, the movement rippling across his fur like the wind. "One cannot miss what one has never had."

I'd enjoyed the love of my father and Nounou. I missed Father now; I had missed Nounou every day since she had died. But I did not wish to throw myself into the ocean for loss of them. That kind of love I shared only with Will. Yet if I had never met him, found such desperate love, would I have longed for it?

I did not know.

"You have a husband, lady?"

Something in Caliban's voice made me glance quickly his way. But he stared at a spate of leaves stuck to his foreleg. He gave them a tentative lick then spat them into the flames.

I wasn't sure what to say. I'd *had* a husband. But he was dead. However, Caliban did not wait for my answer but continued, "I would say you have a husband you must love dearly considering your words."

I had not loved Reginald. In truth, I had loathed him. But I did not wish to speak ill of the dead.

"I have so loved," I said.

"And having loved, you do not wish to return to said husband at the next opportunity?"

"My husband is dead."

"I . . . uh . . ." Caliban blinked. "I am sorry for your loss."

"As am I." Amazingly, my words sounded sincere. I *could* be sorry for Reginald's loss now that he was forever lost.

"How did it happen?"

His gaze was fixed so intently on my face, I looked down. "He was on the ship."

"And became a zombie."

This had not occurred to me. I had not seen him among those I had killed, but Will had killed a slew. However, would he not have told me if he'd ripped off the head of my dead husband?

That I was uncertain disturbed me.

"Mayhap," I agreed. "But if so, he is gone. The island has been cleared of the fiends."

"Not completely," he muttered.

"There are more?"

He lifted his snout to the wailing night. "There will be."

He was right. I set my hand upon my sword and stroked the hilt. "I will end them too."

"You are a hunter?"

"I am."

"How long have you been so?"

"Since I was very young."

"Your husband must have been an amazing man to allow the future mother of his children to risk her life in such a way."

His words took me back to the life I had led with a man who had cared only for the children he could get upon my body. Children who would be heirs to the kingdom he would make with my father's money. He had never cared about me. Not that this made Reginald different from any other man in England. The problem had been that I was different from any other woman.

"He did not know," I said.

"A fool, then?"

"Nay," I said slowly, though there had been a time when I had thought so. "He spent most of the year in Virginia, managing a plantation, and I am very good at dissembling."

My words appeared to surprise Caliban again. "Why would you not tell the man you loved the truth?"

"He was not the man I loved."

Caliban gasped. "You loved *another*?"

"I could not help it. Love is love. It cannot be forced to exist where there is none, nor made nonexistent once it has bloomed. Love just is."

Caliban's fur crumpled as his forehead creased. "Did your poor husband discover your perfidy?"

"He did."

"Did he beat you?"

"He would have. But I have the queen's ear." I lifted my weapon. "And a ready sword."

"Poor man. To be across the sea in a strange, wild land, missing his wife, then to come home and discover her tupping another."

"Which was why I arranged my own death."

Caliban stilled. "What say you?"

Quickly I told him of the plan Will had devised and how it

had gone so wrong. Why I felt the need to confess to him, I knew not. Mayhap it was something in those eyes.

"You not only cuckolded your husband with a common playwright, but allowed the man to mourn your death so you could continue?"

"Will Shakespeare is hardly common," I snapped. I had heard the same before, and I had not liked it overly much then. "And my husband did not mourn my death. He loathed me as much as I loathed him."

"'Twas still bad form to trick the man."

"'Twas for his own good as well as mine own."

Caliban's head tilted, doglike. "How so?"

"He had his title and my wealth. He could marry again. A woman who wanted what he did."

"So you did it all for him?"

"No," I admitted. "I did it for myself. That he would benefit was merely a happy accident."

Those eyes that seemed both familiar and so strange met mine. "You are the coldest woman I have ever known."

"Then you have not known so very many."

I wasn't cold. Or at least I hadn't been once I knew what true warmth could be.

"Why did you dislike your husband so?"

"He made it quite easy." Caliban's head tilted in the other direction, and I found myself explaining again. Mayhap because he'd thought me cold. Mayhap because I feared he was right.

"He wooed me with pretty words, made me believe that he loved me."

"What gall!"

I ignored the sarcasm. I had ignored much worse than that. "Once we were married, the pretty words disappeared. I learned that I was nothing more than a means to his end. Wealth, a barony, and a child."

"Many marriages have been made on less."

"So I have heard. But to be tricked into believing I was special, that I was loved, and to find out otherwise was difficult."

"You were safe, taken care of. I doubt you ever slept upon the ground." Caliban's lip lifted. "Until now."

"He never wasted an opportunity to tell me how I disappointed him." I lifted my hand to my hair. "My hair and eyes were too dark, my skin dun. My breasts too small, my person too tall. In a word—or ten thousand—I was not the fashion."

To a girl who had so badly wanted to be loved, and who had believed she was, the rebukes had been devastating.

"Bad form," Caliban murmured. "Did you share with him your unhappiness?"

"That was the first time he locked me in my room without food or drink." The creature flinched as if he had been the one doing the locking. I shrugged. "'Twas not the last."

"You lied about who you were. You did not tell him of the zombies and of your hunting them."

"You think he would have believed? He would have confined me for the rest of my life. When I am not about in the London night, sirrah, people die!"

Caliban nodded, expression—if a snout could have an expression—grave. "Did you consider, mistress, that he might not have known any better?" At my confused frown, he continued. "Mayhap he was raised in an unfeeling home. How could he behave with love if he never knew such himself?"

I pondered this. "His mother did not seem to have much affection for him. His father was a hard man. Angry over the loss of their fortune. Desperate to build it anew." I nodded

slowly. "As I recall, they didst berate him about his appearance."
Poor man. He could not help how he looked. "Weak chin. Big
nose. He possessed an unfortunate mole."

"You do not think your husband's behavior understandable
considering?"

"I see now the reasons for it," I agreed. Nevertheless—"The
why does not excuse the what. The man tormented me; he im-
prisoned me; he hit me—"

Caliban stiffened. "He did . . ." The creature paused, drew
a breath, continued: "What?"

"Once," I allowed. "He hit me once." But once had been more
than enough.

"He should not have," the beast said quietly.

"He hit me, but he never kissed me. Do you not find that
strange?"

"Did you tell him you wanted a kiss?"

I lifted my fingers to my mouth and thought of the first
time Will had touched his lips to mine, the first time any man
had. "I did not know."

"If he saw the situation from your side"—the monster again
hung his head—"he would be ashamed."

Knowing Reginald, I doubted that. However, Caliban's words
had caused me to see Reginald's point of view, and I had begun
to regret a few things. Mayhap Reginald would as well.

If he weren't dead and past the point of remorse.

A tremendous clap of thunder shook the earth, the mountain, my teeth. Caliban yipped and leaped across the distance
separating us, landing half in my lap. He was shaking.

"Shh," I murmured, drawing my palm down his back. "'Tis
all right."

He did not stop shivering; instead he began to pant.

"How now!" I said. "A mere tempest cannot hurt one such as you."

He stared out the opening. "This storm seems much worse than the other."

"We will be safe. We will not come to harm."

"Until the zombies arrive."

"Fear them not." I smoothed my hand over him again. "I am here."

He craned to peer at me, and I was struck again by his eyes. I could swear that I recognized them. But how could that be?

"Lady," he rumbled, his voice that of no one, nothing I'd ever known, "how can you be so gentle with a beast?"

"Beast is in the eye of the beholder." I *did* love with all my heart what most would consider a bloodsucking fiend.

"The sorcerer said my evil inside would be visible to all now upon my outside," Caliban murmured. "Then I was like this."

"Were you evil?"

He stared into my face as if searching for the answer, then whispered a broken "yes."

"You do not look so horrible to me." I rubbed his snout.

Grateful, he licked my hand.

Lightning exploded at the entrance of the cave. Bright silver sparks bounced off the stone above our heads, slammed into the dirt near our feet, spun through the air past my nose.

Ariel's voice, louder than the thunder, poured from the heavens. "What is the meaning of this?"

As the earth began to rumble, I understood why Ariel had been asking me all those questions about love.

I removed my hands from Caliban's fur, then skittered away, making sure no part of me touched any part of him.

Too late.

The very air crackled, snapping against my cheeks, my arms, and my neck like bees. Then the ground opened and swallowed me whole.

Chapter Twenty-seven

"The winds did sing it to me."

—*The Tempest* (Act III, scene 3)

"Ariel!" Caliban shouted. "No!"

But the fury within her at the sight of her diamond and her monster in each other's arms exploded into action. They must be separated.

Now.

Katherine disappeared, screaming, into a fissure in the earth. Her hands groped at the edge; she nearly pulled herself out. Then Ariel snapped her fingers, and the cleft in the ground closed. The silence after all the rumbling and the yelling made her ears ring.

"What have you done?" Caliban whispered.

"What have you?"

"I spoke with my wife."

"That appeared more than mere speech to me."

"The storm . . ." He looked away, hunched his shoulders. Did she actually hear him whine?

"What of it?"

"It frightened me!" he roared.

Ariel's belly, which had been blazing with a heat she thought might turn her silvery skin scarlet, suddenly tightened then tumbled. The storm was of her making, and she felt . . .

She wasn't sure. She had never felt so before.

She waved her hand, and the storm did still. "Better?"

He lifted his eyes. "Aye."

Ariel considered what she had seen. Caliban lying in his wife's lap, her shift transparent from the rain. Her hand upon his fur, stroking. The calm, content expression upon her face. The budding adoration on his.

"Bring her back," Caliban ordered.

Ariel's stomach, which had begun to settle, blazed. "You told me you did not love her. That she lied to you; she cuckolded you."

"I do not want her dead."

"Why not?"

He hung his head. "I lied to her first. I pretended at love." He lifted blue, brimming eyes. "I did not know any better."

His tale matched the diamond's. But what did that mean?

She was so confused. And angry. Just thinking of Katherine's hand on his head made her want to do violence.

"Bring her back," Caliban repeated.

Ariel merely laughed.

"You need her to kill the zombies your lunatic *master* will soon raise."

"I have you for that. And the vampire. I do not need her at all." Ariel studied his face. 'Twas difficult to decipher his expression beneath the fur, but she thought his human gaze held both fear and fury. "Why do you care?"

"We spoke, and I saw myself through her eyes." His head hung. "I wronged her. I was an evil, selfish man."

His words of understanding for a woman he had previously disliked, and regret for what he had done to her, made Ariel's belly turn to ice, which she understood no more than the fiery heat. "You want your wife back?"

"Aye," he agreed. "Lift her up."

"By the by," she murmured.

"She will die!"

"Death is not what it used to be."

Caliban's upper lip lifted—a snarl without sound. "You would raise her to be a fiend?"

"I am not the one who does the raising."

"Merely the killing."

"I did not kill you." Ariel's gaze narrowed. "Yet."

His snarl gave way to curiosity. "Can I be killed?"

"Of course. You are man and beast. Neither one is immortal."

"But you are?"

Ariel shrugged. So far, nothing on this earth had permanently harmed her. But who knew what the next tide might bring.

"Katherine merely comforted me in the storm," Caliban murmured. "It made me guilty that she could be so kind after all I had done to her."

"What is 'guilty'?"

"'Tis a feeling." He touched his belly. "Here." He lifted his paw to his chest. "Mayhap here."

"It burns," she murmured. "Like flames dancing within."

He shook his head. "Guilt weighs one down. 'Tis gray and chill. A heavy sadness."

"I do not understand feelings." Ariel pouted. "I do not like feeling them."

He moved closer, and she caught his scent. Not dog in a

storm, but fresh rain sparkling upon golden hair. It made her shiver, and silver sparkles cascaded down.

He caught them in his paw. "When did you burn?" he whispered.

Her gaze flicked to his, and those shivers gave way to more heat. The sparkles in his hand turned from silver to gold and then to orange.

"When I saw you with the diamond. Your head pressed to her breasts—"

"Breasts?" he repeated as if he had never heard of them.

"Aye! Your head lay *upon* her breasts."

"She wore clothes."

"Barely. The storm had made her shift translucent."

"I did not notice." She lifted a brow, and he continued, "The only breasts I ever see, Ariel, are yours."

She wanted to believe him, she almost did, but whenever she thought of them together, her insides began to boil.

"Her fingers in your ruff," she said, "and that expression on her face—"

"What expression?"

"She liked you."

Caliban stiffened then coughed—nay, barked—right in Ariel's face. His breath blew back her hair. 'Twas warm and smelled of spice. She moved closer. She could not help it.

"You are mistaken." He lifted a paw. His claw narrowly missed slicing her again. Caliban lowered it then put both arms behind his back. The end of his tail swooshed like a cat's. "Katherine has not liked me in years."

"Did she know you are . . . you?"

"Nay."

Ariel spread her hands. "Then like you she did."

Remembering what she had observed, Ariel curled her fingers into fists. *The diamond should not have touched him thus.* If she were there now, Ariel might have sent her somewhere much worse than into the earth.

"You did not like my wife touching me?" Caliban asked.

"I did not."

"Why?"

"Because you are . . ." Ariel's voice trailed off. She lifted her gaze to his and whispered: "Mine."

Chapter Twenty-eight

"But how is it that this lives in thy mind?"

—*The Tempest* (Act I, scene 2)

Will had been searching for Kate for hours. How could one island be so very large?

He paused, turning in a circle, peering at the trees, the fronds, the flowers. Had he been past this place before?

Will sighed. *Most likely.*

'Twas not as if he had the aid of familiar streets or large ancient landmarks as he did in London. Here, everything appeared the same.

Will had called; Kate had not answered. But the storm raged, worse tonight than any that had come before, and mayhap Kate had not heard him.

Will was drenched. If his blood hadn't already been eternally cold, he would be shivering from the chill of the wind. He worried about his love, dressed in nothing but her shift, feet bare, warm blood turned to ice when surrounded by this tempest.

Will's teeth fair hummed from the thunder; his hair did ache from the lightning. Ariel was in fine form. Many dead would litter the beaches come the morrow.

He had to find Kate before Prospero raised them. They fought better together than apart. And with the number of zombies the old fool would no doubt lift after such an incredible storm, Will feared Kate would be unable to triumph without him.

If he gave in to Kate's request and made her like him, he would no longer have to fret every night that he might lose her, fear that when he slept the sleep of the undead something lethal could befall her, that he would awaken and discover his un-life over because Kate had ceased to exist.

"You cannot," he murmured, and turned in what he hoped was a new direction before plunging into the fray.

Nay, he *would* not.

An hour later he still had not located her. Where could she be?

Will paused again, scowling at what he swore was the same damn tree he'd scowled at not so long before. He hadn't found Kate, but he hadn't found anyone else either. Not Caliban, Ariel, the lunatic Prospero, or a single shambling corpse.

Suddenly the air stilled; the rain stopped as if the bucket from whence it poured had finally emptied. The thunder abated, and the lightning weakened. With his superior hearing no longer encumbered by the *whoosh* and wheeze of the wind, Will thought he detected a voice.

"Vampire! Vampire, I say. Come forth!"

How had Prospero discovered what he was? And what could the fellow want?

Will considered ignoring the summons, but he was curious.

In the next instant, Will ran through the jungle in the direction of the sorcerer's shouts. Because of his amazing vampire speed, he reached his destination in an instant, arriving in front of Prospero as the old man once more drew breath to bellow. At the sight of Will—who no doubt seemed to have appeared from thin air—Prospero let out the breath and opened his arms.

"There you are!"

Will, afraid Prospero meant to hug him, stepped out of reach then glanced around. "We are alone?"

Prospero dropped his arms. "Of course. Our business is for no one's ears but our own."

"What business?" The last time he'd seen Prospero, the lunatic had tried to cast a spell on him. Will wanted no more of the same.

"I hear that you are a vampire."

"How did you hear?"

"It is a small island; people talk."

"There are no people on this island." Except for Kate, but that was for Will to know and Prospero never to find out. Unless the sorcerer had come across Kate and made her tell.

Will was across the short distance between them in a trice. He wrapped his hand around the old man's throat and squeezed. "Where is she?"

Prospero's lips moved, but no sound came out. Will let him go. "If any harm has come to her . . ."

"No harm can come to Ariel; she is a sprite. Fear not."

If the fellow thought Will was asking about Ariel, he must not yet know of Kate. All to the good.

Though the sorcerer had said he'd heard of Will's true nature from a person, that may have been a mere figure of speech. Caliban knew the truth, though why would he speak to Prospero at all? The man had made him into a monster.

Most likely Ariel had seen Will tearing the heads off

zombies—he had not exactly been discreet—and put two and two together to make the inevitable four. Then she'd told Prospero.

Damn fairy.

But Ariel would not have told her master about Kate, as Kate and her reasons for being here would cause as many problems for Ariel as it would for her diamond.

"This book"—Prospero held up the tome that never seemed to leave his clutches—"tells of a being that can raise zombies beneath the light of the full moon."

If Will had yet breathed, the old man's words would have made him stop. "*You* raise zombies," he managed.

"Aye. But the spell requires fortitude, vitality, magic. It exhausts me. I lift all the dead that I can, but then they must have sustenance, which requires brains. Then those who are the sustenance cannot become soldiers. And so on and so forth." He searched Will's eyes. "If I am to have my army, I will need assistance."

"I no longer do that," Will snapped.

Prospero's earnest demeanor vanished before his exuberant smile. "I knew you were a necromancer." He shot a fist into the air. "I knew it."

Fool!

By saying he "did that" no longer, Will had admitted to "doing that" at one time. Add his zombie-raising talent to his vampire identity, and necromancer—a special type of vampire that could raise the dead beneath the full moon—was the result.

"It matters not what you know." Will turned, planning to search once more for Kate.

"If you help me, vampire, then I will help you."

"There is nothing that I need."

An instant before Will would have disappeared into the foliage, the old man murmured, "Not even to be human again?"

Will paused, but he did not turn around. "'Tis impossible."

Prospero laughed. "How can such a word pass your lips? Thou art immortal. I created a caliban. We have both lifted the dead back to life."

Will turned. "That is not life."

"It is not death either." Prospero waggled his book. "What if I possessed a spell that would make you mortal again?"

"Why would I want to be mortal?"

He did, but the reason was Kate and that was his secret.

"Poor boy." The old man shook his head; he even *tsk*ed. "Why would you want to be like this?" His mouth twisted. "Drinking blood. Never gazing upon the sunrise. All those you once knew and loved have died. Anyone you now know or might love will meet the same fate. Does it not grow old? Have you not pined for the life you lost? Would you not like to get it back?"

Will's gaze narrowed. "What if I did?"

"'Tis a simple matter. You give me what I want, then I will give you what you want."

Will was shaking his head before Prospero finished his sentence. He had sworn never to raise another zombie army. He had seen firsthand the destruction they wrought. Kate would never forgive him if he went back to the way he had been.

Even if he went there for her.

Chapter Twenty-nine

"At least bring forth a wonder."
—*The Tempest* (Act V, scene I)

Reginald could not breathe; he could not speak. All he could do was look into Ariel's eyes and feel. She had said he was hers, and oh, how he wanted to be.

He reached for her; she stepped quickly back, avoiding, barely, another lethal slice of his claws. Reginald stared at his paws in disgust. "I will never be able to hold you in my arms without hurting you."

"You wish to?" Ariel's voice was breathless; her breasts rose and fell as fast as the beat of a hummingbird's wings. "Hold me?"

"Aye." He inhaled deeply—relishing her scent, which was moonlight on water, spun sugar at Christmas, spring after winter has fled. "I wish to kiss you, but with this . . ." He tapped his snout with one of the offensive claws. "I would only leave drool upon your chin."

The brilliant blue of her eyes seemed to pulse. "Move not," she whispered, and flitted closer.

He had to grit his teeth to keep from reaching out. She was so smooth and silver. Would her skin be cool, or would it reflect the heat that bubbled even now in his blood? He would never know, because as he was, he could never, ever touch. A growl rumbled in his throat.

"Hush. 'Twill be all right."

"How can it? I am neither man enough to love nor beast enough to hate."

"You are Caliban," she said. "A new creature of which there is only one. You are special. Unique."

Reginald blinked. He had never been unique before. No one had ever thought him special.

Several thuds from behind made Reginald spin about. Apparently the idea of being special had caused his tail to wag. The uncontrollable appendage had brushed a gaggle of items from the nearest table onto the ground.

Clumsy oaf. He was not special at all.

"'Tis nothing," Ariel said briskly. "A miniature of his mother, a few trinkets from the isle." She waved a hand and everything that had been in the dirt floated back onto the surface from whence it had fallen.

Ariel drew her finger slowly through the air in front of Reginald's chest. Sparkles whirled. Both hot and cold, they brushed his fur. He forgot all about his tail.

"The sight . . . ," she began, then paused. Someone was coming.

"Damn vampire!"

Prospero. The voice was unmistakable.

Ariel hissed. Reginald wanted to. He glanced frantically about the cave for a place to hide. The old man was too close for them to escape through the door.

"Right in the middle of a business discussion, he falls dead asleep," the sorcerer ranted.

Reginald stepped toward the rear of the cavern, hoping for a dark corner in which to lurk, but Ariel set her hand upon his paw and shook her head.

"He will see us," Reginald whispered.

"So?"

"He did this"—Reginald indicated his tail—"for less."

"Trust me," Ariel said. "I will not let him hurt you again."

And because he did trust her, because she had her hand on his paw and she left it there as if his paw were truly an arm, and because he had nowhere else to go, Reginald stayed.

"But the sun is up," the old man continued, "and that is the trouble with vampires. Sun up, they go down." A disgusted exhalation trailed free. "'Tis fortunate I do not need him until the moon rises tonight." He muttered a few unintelligible words and then continued. "I could have threatened him with what I knew. But that is a good way to get my throat torn out." He clucked. "No. Better to insinuate. To entice. To hint. Then wait."

The long, broad shadow of a man, thrown forward by that just risen sun, spread across the cavern floor, casting across Reginald's toe-claws. He held his breath, closed his eyes, and waited for the shouts, then the spells, to begin.

Instead, Reginald's face warmed; water crashed, and a fresh, dewy breeze stirred his fur. He could swear he was no longer in the cave but—

Reginald opened his eyes. Both he and Ariel stood at the secluded waterfall where he had seen his wife and Will Shakespeare—

"The sight of lovers feedeth those in love." Ariel moved close enough that the slight chill of her skin refreshed him in the heat.

Did she know what he'd been thinking? Or was she merely remembering that she had seen them too?

"I did not understand." She traced her finger near his fur again, not touching, yet still he stirred. "They kissed, and it looked so . . ."

Her tongue, bright pink against her silver lips, shot out. Reginald wanted to touch that tongue with his own. How strange. He had never wanted to kiss Katherine, never had in truth, and the thought of touching tongues—

He shuddered, but not with disgust. Instead he felt a touch of—

"Temptation." Reginald stared at Ariel. "Lips on lips. Tongues. Delicious."

Delicious. Aye. He was intrigued. However—

"I cannot." He motioned to his horrible snout with his horrible claws. The idea of pressing his beastly mouth-nose to her pert silvery lips, of touching her sly pink tongue with the long, lolling thing that was his—

"Close thine eyes," she whispered. Reginald simply stared. "Trust me." She set her hand upon his paw once more. "You shall see."

"How can I see if mine eyes are closed?"

She smiled. "Then you shall feel."

He remembered how his fur had stirred without a single touch. "Magic?" he asked.

"Shh." She drew her palm in front of his eyes, and they closed. "The sight of lovers feedeth those in love," she repeated.

For an instant he saw again his wife in Shakespeare's embrace, their bodies entwined. But it had not been the sex that aroused him so much as the tenderness, the need, and the desire he'd witnessed between them for each other.

"She was empty," Ariel murmured. She removed her hand from his arm, yet he could swear her fingers yet stroked. "Then she was filled, as only he could fill her."

"Aye," Reginald agreed. "Only he."

Only me, he thought. *Only you.*

"Only me," Ariel whispered. "Only you."

She kissed his lips—when had he regrown lips?—then her tongue, cool and sweet, stroked his. And his tongue did not loll from his mouth, or dribble drool across her chin, but stroked hers with a talent the appendage had not possessed even when it had yet been human.

"Thy hands upon my breasts," she whispered.

And though he did not move, Reginald felt those exquisite silver breasts, soft and cool, round yet firm, the nipples like pebbles against palms he no longer had.

Her gasp of arousal caused his own to spike. He had not known a man's —or a beast's—nipples could do so.

"Fill me," she begged. "Make what is half now whole."

Her hand closed around him, and he hardened in an instant, his entire body drawn to that place where they would fit together like the final two pieces of a puzzle.

He slid within, the walls of her chamber moist, hot, even as her hands on his neck were blessedly cool.

"More," she whispered. "Harder. Faster. Now."

He could not deny her, especially since he wanted nothing more himself than—

Harder. Faster. And now.

His body fair tingled as it had never tingled before. He felt both lively and serene, filled to the brim in places he had never before understood were empty.

He, who had thought kissing unnecessary, sex a mere chore—wet, messy, and base—quickly learned otherwise. Because what he had with Ariel was none of those things.

What he had with her was everything.

Chapter Thirty

"To do me business in the veins o' the earth."

—*The Tempest* (Act I, scene 2)

Dirt and pebbles filled my mouth as I screamed. I snapped my lips closed and attempted to breathe. I inhaled dust and mud but little air.

Ariel had killed me.

As I had recently entertained the idea of dying, my sudden desire to live should have been surprising. However, I had not planned to die beneath the earth.

Buried. Alone. Lost forever.

I needed to die aboveground. Visible. Findable. Able to be lifted again.

The only way to do that was to fight free. Fortunately, like any good *chasseur,* I had kept hold of my sword.

Unfortunately, when one is surrounded by dirt, a sword does little good. My arms and legs were trapped. I could barely twitch a finger, let alone swing a weapon. After a few moments of useless struggling, which only seemed to push me farther away from the surface rather than nearer, I faced the truth.

I would die here, and all my fine plans would come to naught.

I'd known death would come for me. I just hadn't thought it would come so soon. Or like this.

If I'd been a vampire, I would have had no need to breathe; my amazing vampire strength would have freed me from my confines in an instant.

But I wasn't a vampire, and now I would never be.

I stopped fighting and consciousness slipped away. I knew not how long I remained in that state, or even what that state was. Fading life? Near death? Death itself?

Sleep. Sleep at last.

Then dirt sifted across my face. The hint of a breeze. Warmth. The sound of waves. From what had once been complete and utter darkness, there glowed a tiny bit of light.

Heaven?

I would think so, except the light was more orange than white and danced like flames across the vista of my mind.

Hell?

That hardly seemed fair. Then again, what had fair ever had to do with anything?

I became steadily warmer. If not for the light breeze, I thought I would catch fire.

Wait a moment . . .

"Breeze?"

Mine own voice—albeit garbled from the dirt and pebbles within. I spat, drew breath . . .

I could breathe!

My eyes snapped open. I lay on a beach, the bright glow of the midday sun upon me explaining both the extreme heat and the orange wash that had danced beyond my closed eyelids.

The sun shone directly above. How long had I been beneath? And how had I survived?

I sat up. All the other bodies upon the beach did too.

"Hell," I murmured.

Mayhap I *had* died after all.

However, the others were moving more slowly than me. I'd already leaped to my feet, sword in hand. My stomach rumbled, but the idea of fresh brains was ever unappealing.

"Mary, Mary, quite contrary, how does your garden grow," I muttered, voicing a rhyme that had been bandied about after Queen Mary's death. No one would have dared bandy it while she was yet alive and risk the use of the "silver bells and cockleshells," instruments of torture common to Bloody Mary's reign. As I could say more than "brr," and think it too, I must yet be alive.

The zombies came to their feet and turned in my direction. There were perhaps a dozen. More than I could handle alone. I considered it fate, an answer to the question.

Should I die or shouldn't I?

Chapter Thirty-one

"Worse than any death."
—*The Tempest* (Act III, scene 3)

Will awoke to the sun throwing lacy patterns across his face. He frowned at the fronds that shielded him.

The last he remembered, he had been listening to Prospero, who spoke with serpent's tongue of things Will dared not hope.

A spell in his book. Will made mortal again. All he need do was—

Raise another zombie army.

Will rubbed a hand over his face. Had he refused? He could not recall. He remembered the offer, the tickle of temptation that had followed the sorcerer's words. Fighting that temptation had caused him to forget the approach of the sun. When it had burst over the horizon, Will had fallen dead at the man's feet.

At least Prospero had dragged him into the shade, though not, Will was sure, because of any kindness on the old fellow's part. Prospero had kept Will alive—or as alive as Will got—for his own wicked purpose. A purpose Will would not—could not—succumb to.

"Kate!" he shouted. He still did not know where she had gotten to, and he did not like it. Since they had first met, the longest they had been apart was during the few days that encompassed their plot to fake her death.

That having gone so well, Will was understandably nervous.

He listened with his powerful vampire ears, but he did not hear his name called with equal fervor. However, he did detect a certain buzzing.

Bees? No. 'Twas different. Somewhat familiar. The sound of a crowd, mayhap. Murmuring as they awaited the coming entertainment.

He tilted his head. Not quite. The murmurs sounded less like words and more like—

Zounds!

'Twas a crowd all right. A crowd of zombies!

Will sped in the direction of the distant "brr!" How could he not have recognized it? His only excuse, he was half-asleep, and the waves did crash upon several shores, confusing him.

Also, in the back of his mind, he'd believed Prospero would wait to hear Will's answer before raising any more fiends. If Will could lift hundreds of the living dead with a mere pull of his mind beneath the full of the moon, why would Prospero bother to raise any more at all?

Of course, the full moon was days away, and the storm had already been in force, the ships sinking, the dead on their way. If Will had been thinking of anything other than himself, he would have realized that the old man wouldn't be able to leave perfectly good dead bodies upon the beach. What if Will refused the sorcerer's offer—which he damn well planned to do? Prospero would need to continue raising the dead if he ever planned to have enough zombies for an attack.

Will hoped that the herd of fiends had not yet found Kate, or she had not yet found them. She knew better than to fight more than a handful herself. Then again, 'twas an island. How far could she run? Where could she hide?

Mayhap where she'd hidden from him thus far. He prayed she remained there, but Kate had never been one to stay out of sight when the *tíbonage* were about.

Will continued on. The volume of the murmurs *decreased* the closer he came. Because of that strange realization, Will slowed whilst still in the jungle, approaching cautiously.

Particles of ash flickered past his head, and he understood. The volume had decreased because the number of zombies had.

Kate was already here.

The *whoosh* of her weapon, which caused an outraged "brr!" to be cut off mid-"rrr!" revealed her still at work. Only two zombies remained. One drew close to Kate. The other waited politely for her to finish.

Will lifted his eyes heavenward. No one had ever said zombies were the sharpest swords in all of Christendom.

As Kate appreciated Will's confidence in her abilities, he hung back and watched his love work. If he'd rushed in and yanked free the head of the remaining fiend when no yanking was necessary, he would only have increased her already considerable irritation with him.

Aware that another zombie awaited her attention, Kate whacked off the head of the one in front of her at the first opportunity. The creature crumbled into a pile of ashes across Kate's bare feet.

Will folded his arms, lips curving, as he waited for her to eliminate the final threat with a quick backhand. She was so very good at this. Watching Kate kill was like observing a dancer upon the stage—graceful and true—a wonder to behold.

Which was why Will merely stood there gaping when she dropped the blade, tilted her face to the sun, and ignored the clacking teeth of the zombie as it went for her throat.

Chapter Thirty-two

"O you, so perfect and so peerless,
are created of every creature's best!"

—*The Tempest* (Act III, scene 1)

Ariel's stomach fluttered as she waited for Caliban to open his eyes. Had he felt what she had?

Nay. 'Twas impossible. For what she had felt was . . .

Beyond the realm of words.

His eyes opened; she feared he would run. She wanted to. Instead, his gaze captured hers.

"That was wonderful," he murmured. "Exciting. Arousing. Fulfilling. Calming. Peaceful. Captivating."

Mayhap 'twas *not* beyond the realm of words—at least for him.

"And not at all sticky," he finished.

The just born smile upon her lips died. "Sticky?"

"All of the good with none of the bad."

"Bad?" Now her lips did frown.

"Not with you! Nay. Never!"

"You have done that with another?" The wind began to stir; in the distance, lightning crackled from a clear blue sky.

"No! How could I?" She tilted her head, and he murmured: "Why would I?"

The wind stilled, and the sky returned to a serene blue. Caliban blew a quick, sharp breath from his snout. "I have touched my wife and none other."

"None?" Ariel did not know much of men, but she thought they often touched more women than their wives.

"One," he admitted. "But she did not count." His upper lip lifted, revealing sharp, pointy teeth. "I had to pay her." He shifted a furry, golden shoulder. "I was ugly," he said. "No woman wished to kiss me. Ever."

"Ugly is as ugly does," she said primly.

"Until I came here, became this, I was both."

Suddenly Ariel understood what Kate had meant when she'd said: *Sometimes a man is more of a monster than a monster could ever be.*

"If you were so repugnant," Ariel continued, "then why did my diamond marry you?"

"I courted her with words. She was ever enamored of them." He gave a sharp laugh. "Which might explain her behavior with Shakespeare."

"Aye," Ariel agreed. "But I doubt a woman such as she would give her life for words, however pretty."

"Her father sold her, or mayhap mine sold me. It matters not. She had wealth; I had the bloodline."

"Bloodline?"

"I am the distant relative of an earl."

"I do not understand humans."

"Neither do I," he muttered. "It all seems foolish now."

"Explain to me why you touched only one woman before your wife."

Considering the ecstasy that had passed between the two of them, Ariel would think that human men—and women, for that matter—would be unable to stop themselves from repeating that feeling wherever, whenever, and with whomever they could.

"She laughed." Caliban winced. "'Twas horrible."

"The laughter?"

"And the mess. I did not care for it."

"You seemed to care for it quite well. With me."

Where once he had seemed puppylike, clumsy, both sweet and foolish, the glance he gave her now was all wolf—smooth, sleek, a little dangerous.

"That was different," he said. "And you know it."

Since she did, Ariel merely smiled.

"How did you . . . ," he began. "I mean, where did you . . ." He huffed again. "Have *you* done that with another?"

"No!"

"Then how could you know how?"

"I spoke with Katherine."

"Katherine?" He blinked as if coming awake. "How could I have forgotten? You must—"

"I have. She is safe. Fear not."

He opened his mouth, then closed it once more. "If you say it is so, then it is so."

Ariel, used to questions and mistrust, was unsure what to do with acceptance and blind belief beyond accepting it herself.

"How would Katherine know of . . ." He paused, uncertain as she of what to call what had just passed between them.

"Not of this." Ariel flicked her hand back and forth, and a shower of tiny stars fell, bouncing against the grass then into the water, where they sizzled. "But of love, lust, and what they lead to." She shrugged. "She did know quite a lot. Pretty words that said little while explaining much."

"Shakespeare," Caliban growled.

"She learned of love and lust with him, and glad you should be of it too."

His growl rumbled louder.

"Hush!" She tapped her finger atop his snout, and he inhaled so sharply he sneezed. "Without her knowledge, we would have never had this. And was not this worth all that has come before?"

"It was," he agreed, albeit sullenly.

"You said no one had ever touched you like I had."

"No one had. Not even when I was yet a man." He glanced downward. "Especially when I was yet a man."

"How did I touch you?"

He hesitated long, then whispered: "As if you wanted to."

Her chest warmed; her throat went thick. She wasn't sure she could speak, but she did. "No one had ever looked at me like you did."

His gaze came up, confusion flickering in the beautiful blue depths. "How?"

"As if I were Ariel, female not fairy, as if you cared for *me* and not for what I could bring you."

Silence fell between them, broken only by the tumble of the waterfall at their backs.

"I burned," Ariel continued. "In here." She set her palm to her belly. "Softly when you touched me, like a tiny flame within the dark of night. But higher, deeper, angrier, whenever I thought of—"

He moved closer; his fur brushed her naked thigh, causing gooseflesh and sparkles. He kept his paws behind him, his shoulders bunched, as if he were holding on to his claws ever tighter. "I would never willingly harm you, Ariel."

He wanted to touch her as badly as she wanted to touch him. She could do so, but how unfair for her to have that joy and for it to be denied to him. Better to do what worked best for them both—that joyous meeting of the minds that mimicked a sensual meeting of the bodies.

Ariel imagined a lovers' caress—his caress.

Caliban's breath caught; his gaze lifted and, together, they smiled. The smile had a touch all its own. For several long, lovely moments, the two of them stood there and felt each other's touch from their heads to their toes without ever moving any closer at all.

"You said you burned higher and deeper," he began.

"When I thought of you caressing your wife as I wanted you to caress me."

"Jealousy," he said, voice full of wonder.

"I do not understand this word."

"Envy, covetousness, resentment. Wanting what someone else has with a bitterness that consumes." His gaze met hers. "It burns."

"You have felt thus?"

"Aye."

"Because of Shakespeare?"

"Because of him and also before."

"Your wife was always false?"

He considered then shook his head. "I had a friend who whispered into my ear that a woman such as she would never love one such as me. I believed him and behaved badly." He glanced down. "I convicted her without cause, treated her like a prisoner and worse. 'Twas no wonder that when she had the opportunity to stray, she took it."

"'Twas still bad form to hurt you thus."

"It was." He met her gaze. "But now that I know you, I understand her better."

"How so?"

"Once love is found, the chill of a forced marriage would be difficult to endure. How could one resist a lover's embrace?"

"Nigh on to impossible," Ariel agreed. Her shoulders rose and fell. "And even though I know you do not love her, yet still I burn." She lifted her hand as he opened his mouth. "Foolish, I know, but she is your wife."

"She believes me dead, and like this . . ." He waved a claw at his caliban form. "I may as well be. Unless . . ." Then he paused, cocking his head with a wrinkle of his brow.

"What?"

"No. I would not ask. I care not. 'Tis nothing."

"Ask," she ordered.

"You said I looked at you as Ariel, and I do." His eyes caressed. "I do." She had no doubt he spoke true. "So to ask you of your magic, 'tis not right."

"Ask," she said again. "I do not mind."

Still, he hesitated. She might have to use her magic just to make the question tumble free of his snout. But his reluctance caused Ariel to realize that her own words were true.

She did not mind.

"You can bring the storm, remain invisible to humans, fly through the air, and change thy shape?"

"I can."

"With all those powers, I wonder . . ." His gaze intensified. "Can you mend me?"

She frowned, then allowed her gaze to wander from his floppy ears over his snout, his claws, his fur, all the way to his long, bushy tail before she answered.

"Caliban." Ariel set her hand atop his head. "There is nothing in need of repair."

Chapter Thirty-three

"Let it be to-night."
—*The Tempest* (Act III, scene 3)

Rooted to the sand, staring in horror at the snapping jaws of undeath headed straight for his love's throat, Will almost waited too long. Thank heaven for his amazing vampire speed.

He raced forward, quick as a blink, snatching the fiend into his arms, tossing the just-beginning-to-rot bastard over his shoulder, and disappearing into the jungle on the opposite side of the beach before Kate even opened her eyes.

When he reached a clearing far enough away that she could not soon come upon him, Will stopped, dumped the zombie to the ground, and yanked his head free of his neck with a quick, sure flick of his wrists.

Ashes rained, scattering across Will's feet then blowing away. He noticed them not. He was too deep in thought.

What had she been thinking?

He recalled her words to him the last time they'd spoken, right before she had stalked away.

We cannot go on like this, Will. . . . Time passes, things change.

I don't, had been his reply.

Exactly.

She did not want to grow old as he stayed forever young. She wished to be like him, but he had refused. Which suddenly made clear her plan.

"The stroke of death is as a lover's pinch, which hurts and is desir'd," he murmured.

She believed that if she died, he would have little choice but to raise her again, or lose her, truly, forever. He had sworn he would not make her like him, but such was easy to say to her yet breathing face.

Will turned in the direction he'd last seen Prospero. "The devil their virtue tempts," he murmured, heading into the jungle, "and they tempt heaven."

He'd sworn he would not take this bargain, but now . . .

What choice did he have?

Will found Prospero. Eventually. Considering the deserted nature of the isle, and that it *was* an isle, finding whom you were searching for was a lot more difficult than it should be. For a while Will even entertained the notion that the old man could render himself invisible too.

Of course, some of the difficulty lay in Will's reluctance to shout. He did not want to speak with Kate right now. He was furious with her; she was furious with him. They would say things they did not mean, or mayhap say things that they did.

He also did not want her to know of his plan until it was accomplished. Which, he thought, had also been her plan. Once done there was no going back.

Halfway through the afternoon, as the sun fell toward the sea, Will discovered Prospero sitting on a low rock, observing the beach.

"I will do it," Will said.

The old man did not even turn around. "It must be to-night."

"No," Will protested. He needed more time to become accustomed to the idea. Besides— "Only beneath the full moon can I raise the dead."

Now Prospero turned. "Leave that to me."

Will reminded himself the old man was crazy. The moon was still days from full, and there was nothing that could be done about that.

Such knowledge would have calmed Will, if it weren't for the fact that the moon *would* become full and he *would* again raise zombies.

However, just because Will raised the zombies didn't mean he couldn't kill the zombies. Certainly, he would no longer be next to immortal once Prospero fulfilled his part of the bargain, but he could still fight at Kate's side for as long as it took to right the wrong he would make. Then he would have to hope she could forgive him.

Prospero's manic gaze bored into Will's. "You will help me raise all the dead which arrive upon this isle beneath the light of the next full moon?"

"Aye." Will agreed, then allowed his own gaze to bore into Prospero's, but the fellow glanced away.

Damn sorcerer. He was impervious to Will's "push." Will would have had no compunction about ordering the fellow to make Will human, then having the fool forget he had ever met vampire Shakespeare. But he could "push" until his head ached and this man would not bend.

"Once I have done your bidding," Will continued, "you will make me human again?"

Prospero's lips curved. "I will."

And though Will believed this was the best way, the only way, to make things right for him and Kate, still he had the feeling that, somehow, things were about to go very, very wrong.

Chapter Thirty-four

"I have cursed them without cause."
—*The Tempest* (Act V, scene 1)

"Approach, my Ariel. Come!"

Ariel jerked her hand back. Her palm had been very close to Caliban's face. Not touching, yet he had felt her just the same.

She glanced around, but they were alone in the glade. Her master did not know of this place, though that did not prevent his shout from reaching her here.

"Stay," Caliban murmured, his gaze capturing hers more firmly than a hand ever could. All that he felt lay in his eyes, or mayhap merely reflected all that lay in hers.

"Would that I could." Her feet lifted from the ground.

"Do not leave me."

Her toes touched again the soil. "Never."

"Yet you are leaving me now."

"My master calls; I must obey."

"When will you be free of him?"

"Ariel!" Prospero's voice boomed like thunder, and she flinched.

"He promised to release me when his army was complete. When he had enough risen dead to reclaim his throne."

"Then why did you bring a zombie hunter to thwart him at every turn?"

"I could not let him take an army off this isle to kill others who were innocent too."

"You realize that the more zombies Katherine kills, the more Prospero will order you to raise? The innocent will continue to perish."

"I did not know what else to do," Ariel said. "I had hopes he would tire of the game. Or die."

When, oh, when would that old bastard die?

"Ariel! To me!"

"I must go." Ariel touched lips to palm then blew softly across the surface. She saw the moment her kiss reached Caliban's mouth. His eyes drifted closed; his tail did wag. She dashed away before he came back to the earth. An instant later she found Prospero alone on a distant beach.

"Thou didst a wondrous thing, Ariel."

She remained silent. He would continue; she need not ask. The problem had never been getting Prospero to talk; the problem had forever been getting him to stop.

"The vampire has proved a welcome addition."

Ariel's forehead creased. "The vampire who slayed the zombies?"

Prospero turned. "Are there others?"

The truth trembled upon her tongue. She dashed it with another. "There is only one vampire on this isle."

He smiled, and for an instant Ariel feared he knew everything. But if that were the case, he would be shouting; he would be casting spells; he would be putting her back in the tree.

"And that one will prove most helpful," he murmured.

Ariel had not meant to be helpful. However, she could not say so.

The sun hovered at the edge of day, a great orange ball perched upon the vast blue water.

"I will need more," Prospero murmured.

At first Ariel thought he meant more vampires, and panic threatened. A zombie army was bad enough, but an army of vampires—

"Spirit." Prospero motioned toward the sea. "Behold my destiny."

Ariel followed his gaze to the line of ships upon the horizon. More than had ever been there before.

"Drown them all," he ordered.

"Sire," she began, "so many would rot before—"

He began to laugh, a high-pitched, insane cackle that made Ariel's ears ache before he stopped and fixed her with a glare. "Do as I say or find yourself confined to that tree forever."

Ariel lifted her chin, prepared to refuse, and Prospero continued. "Do this for me, spirit, and I will free you before the moon doth rise this night."

Ariel's lips pressed together to keep the treacherous "nay" from escaping. If she were free, she could do many things. Kill zombies herself, for instance, maybe even bring the dead back to life. She would never know unless—

"One last storm," she clarified, "and I am free?"

"One last storm," he agreed.

Ariel lifted her arms and called the wind.

Chapter Thirty-five

"It is foul weather in us all."

—*The Tempest* (Act II, scene 1)

I waited for death, but death did not come.

Tentatively I opened one eye. The sight that greeted me made both fly open.

I stood alone upon the beach.

Mayhap I was already dead, and the fiend had eaten my brains. How could I smell the fragrant scent of rotting zombie tongue wash across my face, hear the clacking of hungry teeth, feel the grope of bony hands, and yet be alive?

Zombies did not know mercy. They were raised for a purpose, and they followed through on the charge from their maker, whatever that might be. Along the way they ate fresh brains whenever fresh brains crossed their paths. They could not help themselves.

So what was the matter with this one?

"Which one?" I muttered.

There wasn't a zombie anywhere near, and once again I was back to dead. Or perhaps crazy. I wasn't sure which I preferred.

Dead and I would have accomplished what I'd planned to. Crazy and I—

"Better dead," I decided. However, I didn't feel dead. Mayhap I was a ghost.

Still dead, but at least Will could see me. We could talk. I'd be able to convince him, if he needed convincing any longer, to make me like him.

I stepped into the jungle, intent on finding my love, then stepped out and scooped up my sword. That I *could* scoop, and the weapon did not fall through ethereal fingers, meant I was yet alive, and if that was the case, I would need something sharp in hand.

I traversed the isle for hours. No sign of anyone but me. At least I did not come across another shambling fiend. I was uncertain if I would have the courage to bare my throat again.

But as the sun fell, the sky turned black; needles of rain attacked in a torrent. The thunder fair shook the earth, and in the distance the wind did wail.

"Nay," I whispered, tilting my head. Those were screams.

I attempted to run toward them, but the tempest became even more violent; I could not distinguish from which direction the cries hailed. The wind was so strong I had to fight against it. 'Twas not long before I sank to the muddy earth then crawled beneath the fickle comfort of a bush. With every sweep of the storm, the leaves parted and dumped more moisture upon me. I hid my face.

I knew not how long I remained there, mayhap I slept at last, then in what seemed the next moment, but could not be, I heard a voice.

"Shake off slumber, and beware: Awake, awake!"

"I am." I lifted my head. The storm was gone as if it had

never been. Stars sparkled across the sky, and though the trees fair dimmed the glow of the moon, the orb still seemed to pour forth more light than it should.

"This is a strange repose," the fairy murmured. "To be asleep with eyes wide open; standing, speaking, moving, and yet so fast asleep."

"I was not asleep." I stood. Although how, then, had the storm passed and I had not noticed it go? I would think that Will had "pushed" me, but he had been nowhere near. Unless he had ordered me not only to sleep but to forget that he had done so.

"Nay," I murmured. He would not. He had promised.

"'Tis neither here nor there," Ariel said. "Come with me. You must stop him."

"Him?" I echoed.

Either I *had* been asleep, heavily and long, or someone had given me another sleeping draught; mayhap they had cast a spell.

"I did as he bade," Ariel continued, "and now I am free. But they are going to raise them all. 'Twould be better, I think, if they did not."

"They?" I repeated. Hadn't she just said *him*?

"Aye," Ariel snapped, more impatient with my slow-witted mimicry than I was, then she transported me to the beach.

Chapter Thirty-six

"You'll lie like dogs and yet say nothing neither."
—*The Tempest* (Act III, scene 2)

Will had returned to the shore as the storm died to discover the sorcerer and the fairy together.

Prospero spread wide his arms, his smile out of place on a beach where dead were stacked like cordwood. "My Ariel, chick, that is thy charge: then to the elements. Be free, and fare thou well!"

The spirit cast Will a quick glance and disappeared.

"Please you." Prospero beckoned. "Draw near."

"Without the full moon I can do nothing." Will picked his way through the dead. "You have wasted the storm, and all these lives, for naught."

Prospero stroked his chin. "Do not trouble yourself."

The waves lapped. The wind whistled. The old man stared at the silvery glow just below the horizon as if he could wish the moon full.

The thought made Will uneasy. What if Ariel could . . . ?

"You have freed the fairy from bondage?" Will asked.

"I did promise to do so once she brought me enough dead for an army."

"As you promised to make me human, once I raised them."

"Aye."

"And she *is* free?"

The old man's eyes did narrow. "Dost thou think I lie?"

"I do not know."

"Ariel!" Prospero shouted. "Come hence! Make haste!"

They waited. The sorcerer called again. They waited some more. When no answer and no fairy were forthcoming, Prospero spread his hands and lifted his red-white brows.

As far as Will knew, bondage meant obedience, and that Ariel ignored the call indicated freedom.

Though Will was heartened to discover Prospero had kept his vow to the sprite, he was also downhearted at what he must do to obtain his own promise from the man.

Not that Ariel had enjoyed her own task any more than Will would enjoy his. If she had, neither Will nor Kate would be here at all.

"You should not have ordered so many deaths this night," Will said. "I can do nothing to help."

"You are wrong," the old man whispered, and the moon slipped over the horizon.

Will frowned, squinting at the apparition as it slowly lifted into the sky. 'Twas impossible, but the orb appeared—

"Full," he said, his voice as dead as the bodies upon the beach.

"Aye," the old man agreed, his voice much more lively.

"How did you do that?" The man had not cast a spell; he had not even opened the book.

"Some talents come from within." He waved his hand, dismissing any further questions. "It matters not how, what matters is that I did what I said I would, and now you must too."

Will had not realized how much he'd been counting on the lack of the full moon to grant him a reprieve until he nearly wept as the silver light fell upon the beach and caused the faces of the dead to glow.

"No one must see me here," Will murmured.

Prospero opened his book, thumbed through several yellowed pages, set his fingertip atop one, and uttered a string of words that might have been Latin. Will knew some Latin but not all. Then the man slapped closed the book, narrowly missing his own finger, and lifted his gaze. "Yon eyes are closed."

"Ariel?" Will asked. "Caliban?"

"Ask what you truly wish to know. If your love sleeps."

"My love?" Will's neck prickled. How had the sorcerer learned of Kate's presence here, and what did it mean?

"Your love, yes," the old man said impatiently. "Do you think I do not know everything that takes place upon mine own isle?"

"I . . . uh . . ."

"I care not if she is here. Right now all I care about is that you are, and that you do as you promised."

"I will. If she cannot see."

"I made all inclined to sleep. 'Tis a good dullness."

"All?" Will asked.

Prospero lifted one shoulder, gaze now rapt upon the dead. "Ariel is strange. There are times when my spells work not upon her." He put his crooked finger to his thin, dry lips in a shushing gesture. "Do not tell."

Will shook his head in both agreement and impatience. "On humans your spells dost work?"

Prospero spread his hands to indicate the rows of the departed. "Dead or alive they respond to my power."

Will wasn't certain how much power the old man had, as he needed Will's help, but his book appeared quite useful. At any rate, Kate should be asleep, and he need not fear her coming upon them and observing his fall from grace. He did not care for the fact that Prospero knew she was here, but he would deal with that later.

Will's distaste for what was to come did not abate with the assurance that no one would see him lift the dead but the sorcerer. What did it matter if Kate saw him raise the zombies or not? The fact would remain that Will had raised them. He would have broken both his vow to himself and his promise to her. He would have to hope that his coming return to humanity would be enough to assuage the guilt and the recriminations.

He let his gaze wander over the hundreds of dead upon the beach, then sighed. He doubted anything would be enough after this.

"The moon blankets them all," Prospero said. "Do thy magic."

Will did not think that what he did was magic, but he had no better word for it. Unless he called it a curse.

When he'd first become a vampire, Will had not known that his inborn affinity for the dead would become amplified with his undeath. Strolling past a graveyard beneath the light of a full moon, he'd been confused when the earth spewed forth its dead.

It had taken time and practice, but eventually Will understood what he had done and learned not to do it unless he meant to. A full moon, the conscious reaching for those that were gone, a little mind pull, and voilà! The dead would walk.

"Shakespeare," Prospero murmured. "Before I die, if you please?"

Will resisted the urge to hurry along the man's demise. What if Prospero was the only one who could work the spells in that book? Will would remain forever a bloodsucking fiend.

The time for hesitation was past. Will had agreed to raise this army. He would do so. Then he would be made human, and he would help Kate end them all.

A simple plan. Those always worked the best.

In theory.

Will lifted his face to the moon, he reached for those who were dead, like him, and he . . . pulled.

'Twas a large number. More than he had ever lifted at one time before. Will tugged until his head did ache.

But, eventually, they rose.

Chapter Thirty-seven

"I will tell no tales."
—*The Tempest* (Act V, scene I)

One moment Reginald awaited Ariel at the waterfall, the next he squatted in the jungle, watching Shakespeare raise zombies. He ducked lower as the very air around him buzzed with an awakening "brrr!"

"Thou ruttish motley-minded varlet!" Reginald muttered.

A soft, horrified gasp made him spin about. Katherine crouched at his side, eyes wide, face white.

"You did not know he could do that?" Reginald asked.

Her head jerked toward him. "Where did you come from?"

"Ariel," he said simply. 'Twas the only way he could have been transported from waterfall to oceanside in an instant.

Katherine's gaze scanned the sky, then the area surrounding them. "Is she here?"

"Nay."

"Damn fairy," Katherine muttered.

Reginald was tempted to defend the sprite, but they had more pressing matters at hand. "Did you know?" he repeated. "That he could raise zombies?"

"Aye. Though he swore he would never do so again."

"He lied," Reginald said simply.

She cast him a quick glance, both suspicion and agony alight in her eyes. "Do you think he was doing so all along?"

Reginald considered his options. He could end forever her love for the fiend. Fuck Shakespeare as Shakespeare had fucked him, or at least fucked Reginald's wife. All he need do was tell her that the playwright had raised the isle's dead. That he, Caliban, had caught the vampire in the act. Or at the least neglect to say that he had seen Prospero raise them as well.

A mere day ago Reginald would have done so. Today he could not.

"He wasn't." Despite Reginald's best intentions, his voice still held a hint of petulance.

"He is." Katherine indicated the beach then shuddered. "He has."

"Tonight. 'Tis true," Reginald agreed. "But the old man was the one who raised them before."

"So Ariel said, but mayhap she lied as well."

"Mayhap," Reginald agreed. "But—"

He hesitated as the temptation toward vengeance again flickered, then set his jaw and blurted: "I saw Prospero raise the others. He used a spell from that book."

Her gaze returned to the zombies, the beach, and the two shadows, black against the rising full moon. She frowned at that moon. "I could swear the moon was yet days from full."

Reginald could have sworn the same.

"That book is a mischief," Katherine murmured.

Reginald touched his claw to his snout. "Aye."

"Thank you for telling me." She tilted her head. Her attention was too probing by half. "You . . . remind me of someone."

Reginald turned away so she could no longer gaze into eyes that, though set in the face of a beast, were the same eyes that had been set in the human face of the husband she had known. "Someone you cared for?"

Why had he asked that? Katherine had never cared for him, and he understood now why. He did not want her to recognize him. He wished she would continue to think him dead and go on about her life, as he would go on about his.

Here.

The revelation was sudden and startling in its clarity. He had no desire to leave this isle. He did not wish to return to the man he had been or the life he had led. He had been miserable, and he had not known it because in all his life he had never experienced true happiness.

Until he had come here.

He had been a monster—ugly both without and within. He was surprised Prospero's curse—*the monstrousness upon the inside, now visible to all upon the outside*—had not left his appearance exactly as it had been rather than turning him into this. He was now a noble beast—the strength of will and body giving birth to a new strength of character. Who would have thought he would need to become a monster to understand what it meant to be a man?

"Aye," Katherine murmured, and Reginald's attention was drawn back to her. "You do remind me of someone I cared for."

For an instant he considered that she might know the truth, but if so, she would have kicked him and not smiled so sadly his chest ached.

She stood, revealing herself to all upon the beach. The familiar murmur—"*Brrr!*"—filled the air as she spun about, then sprinted away.

Reginald glanced toward the ocean, where hundreds of rapt, dead eyes were now fixed on him.

"Uh, Katherine," he said, though she was long gone, "I think we were supposed to kill them."

Chapter Thirty-eight

"It carries a brave form. But 'tis a spirit."

—*The Tempest* (Act I, scene 2)

Kate stood framed by the lush greens and bright orange, yellow, and purple flowers. The scene would be worth painting, if Will painted, and if her face were not ghost white, her dark eyes both horrified and haunted.

As Will's heart did not beat, how, then, could it break?

Before he could say or do anything—although what he might have said or done would forever remain a mystery—Kate was running, disappearing into the trees, while he continued to stand there like one of the creatures he had just raised.

However, the zombies had seen her too, and they surged forward. They could not all fit on the path; the barrier of trees confused them, and they were too stupid to form a line. So the army milled aimlessly upon the sand, bumping into one another and murmuring: "Brr?"

"My army is complete," Prospero announced, "and the throne will soon be mine."

The old fellow was insane. He might possess an army, but the only throne he could take, considering an ocean surrounded them, was the one that would make him king of Zombie Island, and wasn't he that already?

"You told me all who were human lay asleep," Will muttered.

Prospero spread his hands and shrugged. In truth it did not matter any longer. Kate had seen, and now Will must find her and explain.

He took a step after her, but hundreds of shambling corpses stood in his way. So he sped in the opposite direction, before cutting to the right in an attempt to head Kate off. With his amazing vampire speed, Will reached the ocean on the opposite side of the island in moments.

"How now?" he whispered. Where could she be?

He plunged into the jungle once more. Though he knew in his head she had to be somewhere, he feared in his undead heart that he would never find her.

After what he'd witnessed earlier, he feared she might have thrown herself into the jaws of a zombie—there were now plenty available thanks to him.

She would die believing he would raise her, and he could not. Kate did not understand the "rules" of becoming a vampire.

Because he had never told her.

He had not wanted to bring the horror of what he was, what he would always be, and how he had become that, into the beautiful, magical place they had created. But by keeping her ignorant, he had put her at risk.

Would she haunt him as a ghost? Following him throughout eternity, begging him to lift her back to unlife, over and over and over again?

Will shuddered, then bellowed: "Kate!"

Nothing answered but a now gentle wind.

Panicked, he sped through the trees once more, uncaring if

he smashed into one, caring only that he would find her. He eventually slammed into something and landed on his arse.

"You!" Caliban said.

Will rubbed his forehead. "I grow weary of this game."

The creature gingerly probed its snout. "As do I."

"I must find Kate."

Caliban's claw fell back to his side. "She saw."

"I know."

Glancing away, Caliban sighed then glanced back. "There is a cave in the mountain. We—"

Will did not realize he'd begun to snarl until Caliban rolled his eyes. "If you think she played you false with me, then you are a bigger fool than you appear."

He was right.

"I apologize." Will bowed his head. "Continue."

"We once waited out a tempest within Prospero's lair. If I were she, that is where I would go."

"I am grateful," Will said.

"You should be."

There was something about the creature's voice, those eyes.

"Do I know thee?" Will asked.

"I do not even know me," Caliban said, then fell onto all fours and loped away.

Will stared after him for several moments before heading for the mountain, where he stepped into one cave after another, finding each one danker, darker, and emptier than the one before. He began to believe that Caliban had sent him on a wild and merry chase, was even now following behind, choking back laughter at Will's gullibility, then he paused before yet another gaping maw and caught the scent of roses.

He found her huddled next to the fire just past a tumble of

books, a bed, trinkets—sticks, stones, shells, mayhap a miniature—strewn across a table. He did not pause to examine, his gaze captured by the tears glistening on his love's cheeks.

"Why did you do it?" she whispered.

"You do not understand," he began.

Her gaze came up, fierce despite the tears. "You lifted an army, Will, when you swore to me you would never."

"He promised me—"

"*You* promised *me*!"

"I am sorry."

"I trusted you," she said. "I loved you."

"I pray you, do not fall in love with me," Will murmured. "For I am falser than vows made in wine." He had not meant to be false; he had meant to be human.

For her.

"Who promised you?" she asked, then answered her own question. "Prospero. What did he promise?"

"If I would lift an army, then he would make me human."

She looked Will up and down. "You do not look human to me."

He deserved that. "I came after you before he could cast his spell."

"And the moon? How came it full?"

"He controls the moon. At first I did not believe, but—"

"You are a fool."

The coldness in her voice, her face, terrified him. "I did it for you," Will babbled. "So you would not die in an attempt to become a fiend like me."

Her dark gaze cut to his. "You saw?"

"I did. I could not allow that."

"Instead hundreds of others die," she snapped. "Has being undead made you forget the value of human life?"

"The only life that matters to me is yours."

"Then you *are* a fiend as you have so often claimed. How could you? You, who know how horrible a zombie army can be, how history is changed when insanity rules."

"All I could think about was you."

"You lie." Her eyes blazed. "All you could think about was *you*."

"No, Kate—"

"Yes, *Will*."

She stood, her shadow rising against the stone wall like the warrior queen Boudicca, who had fought the Romans. She would have won too, if Will hadn't raised that damn zombie army for Suetonius. He hadn't felt bad about it then—he hadn't known any better—but he certainly did now. He was surprised Boudicca hadn't haunted him, though maybe she had yet to start.

"You have made a pact with the Devil."

Maybe not *the* Devil, but *a* devil.

"Prospero tempted me with something I could not resist."

"You could not resist being party to the death of countless others?"

"I could not turn my back on the promise of a life with you."

She seemed to deflate at his words, shoulders slumped, face canted down.

"The chance to know again the morning sun," he continued. "To walk wherever I wished, whenever I wished." Kate lifted her head, and Will whispered: "With you."

"To die," she returned. "To sleep no more. And by a sleep to say we end the heartache and the thousand natural shocks that flesh is heir to. 'Tis a consummation devoutly to be wished."

"Beautiful," he whispered, wishing for mayhap the thousandth time since he had come upon this isle that his quill did not rest at the bottom of the sea.

She cast him a narrow glare. "If you would but listen to the meaning of the words and not their flow, you would not think them so beautiful. What I am saying, Will, is that if you are human, you will die."

"If you had let that zombie kill you, so would you have."

Confusion creased her face. "You would have raised me." He shook his head. "You would have allowed me to remain dead rather than make me like you?"

"There are rules about vampires, just as there are rules about zombies. If you had died like that, the only way to bring you back would have been as one of them."

"Nay," she whispered, but her voice did tremble.

"To be raised as a vampire . . ." Will paused, not wishing to articulate the truth, but knowing that he must. "You must drink from one as you die."

Kate's lips twisted in disgust. "Drink blood?"

"Thou must get used to it."

"I did not know."

Precisely.

"You behaved rashly, Kate, and you frightened me. When Prospero presented a solution, I took it. I did not think." He waited until her eyes met his. "As you did not think."

"You would rather die with me than live forever like you?"

"I would."

Kate considered his words for several moments, then nodded. The pain in Will's chest eased. Mayhap this could all work out.

"Find the old man," she said. "He need fulfill his half of your devil's bargain." She tilted her head. "If that is what you truly want."

"I do." The idea that his heart might once again beat made Will so light-headed with joy he thought he might succumb to a very human frailty and swoon. "Let us go."

"Not us." Kate stood, sword in hand. "I have zombies to kill."

A winter wind traced his spine. "Not alone. I will help."

"Prospero will not fulfill his part of the bargain if you obliterate yours." She lifted her hand, reading his next thought before it could even leave his mouth. "And you cannot fight them when you are only human."

"You do."

Her back straightened. "I am a *chasseur*."

"I cannot leave you to—"

"You sacrificed hundreds to get back your life. The least you can do is live it."

"The least I can do is make certain no more die because of me."

"We are on an island, Will. The only ones who might die are us."

Will considered. Prospero was human, but zombies did not turn on their maker, and though Will had raised them, he had ordered them to follow the sorcerer's commands. As the zombies had not turned on Prospero and immediately devoured what small amount of food occupied the man's head, Will concluded that his orders had held. The creatures considered Prospero their leader. However—

"There's Caliban," he said.

Concern filled Kate's eyes. "We should find him."

"Or we could remain here until they all die from lack of . . . brrr."

"Ariel will bring"—her mouth pursed—"that."

"Prospero released her from bondage. She is gone."

"I am here."

Will turned just as the fairy's bare feet touched the ground. "He did not free you?" Will's voice went womanish with panic. If the old man had broken his promise to the sprite, then his promise to Will was no doubt shattered as well.

"He did, but I cannot go."

"Cannot?" Kate asked. "Or will not?"

Ariel shrugged. "I chose this isle for my home. I do not wish to leave; I only wish to have it back the way it was. If my diamond wouldst but rid the place of the shambling zombie army, it could be."

"Can you not wave your hand and make them all disappear?" Kate asked, gaze focused above and to the left of where the fairy actually hovered.

"If I could, I would not have brought you here in the first place," Ariel snapped. "He has freed me, but apparently I cannot take back that which I gave to win my freedom."

Kate nodded slowly. "All right. I will clear the isle. Although . . ." Her forehead creased. "If you have brought them no sustenance, they will not shamble about for very long."

"Sustenance," Ariel repeated, then let loose a slew of indecipherable gibberish that, considering her furious tone, could only be fairy curses.

The final two words, spat in the same furious manner an instant before she disappeared, were quite clear.

The ships!

Chapter Thirty-nine

"But 'tis gone.
No, it begins again."
—*The Tempest* (Act I, scene 2)

"What ships?" I shouted, but there came no answer.

I glanced at Will, and he shook his head. Ariel had left.

Just looking at him made my chest ache. I was both angry and sad. When I wasn't frightened, excited, and glad.

Rhyming. I did that only when I was beyond confused. I loved him, but right now I also hated him. Or mayhap I only hated what he had done.

How could I fault him for doing anything to be with me, when I would have done anything for the same reason? His way involved murder, mine suicide. Both sins. Both unforgivable. If we were the type of people bound by such things.

"All the ships that have come within a league of here are at the bottom of the ocean," Will said, his brow creased in thought.

"Not all." Caliban loomed in the opening.

"This cave is busier than opening day at the Rose," I muttered.

Will cast me a silencing glance. "Explain," he ordered the creature.

"At one time Prospero had Ariel bring live brains upon the isle."

"One time," I agreed. "But not this time."

"Because he is taking this army away," Caliban said.

"On the ships that brought the earlier sustenance," Will murmured, then smacked himself in the forehead with the heel of his hand.

"What?" I asked, still not understanding.

"If the ships upon which the sustenance arrived had sunk—"

"All aboard would be dead," I finished.

"Aye," Will agreed. "So somehow he enticed the living onto the isle, then moved the ships elsewhere until he had enough zombies to fill them."

His shoulders slumped; he appeared defeated. I wanted to gather him into my arms and tell him everything would be all right. But I wasn't sure it would be.

"Where?" I asked.

We glanced at Caliban; he spread his paws.

"Think," Will snapped. "You have lurked all over this isle. You must know a place where they could be."

At the word *lurk*, Caliban lifted his lip in a silent snarl, then his head tilted in a doglike manner so at odds with the humanity of both his speech and his actions.

"I have seen no ships. But there is one area I have not explored completely. A deep nook on the far side of this mountain. They could be there."

"Let us go," I said.

Caliban and I headed for the door. I had taken several steps before I realized Will was not with me. I turned to find him staring at something in his palm. His face shone white in the dying firelight, and his eyes when he lifted them to mine blazed frighteningly black.

"What is it?"

He turned his hand. Cupped within lay a miniature. The woman's golden hair shone as brightly as the pearls in her green-and-black headdress. Her gown was fine, the cut of the neckline and the jewels about her throat revealed her quality. Youth shone from her smooth face and danced in her snapping dark eyes.

"'Tis Prospero's mother," Caliban said.

Will nearly dropped the portrait on the ground.

"Who is she?" I whispered.

"Mary." Will's voice came out a croak.

"Tudor?" I frowned. The late king's sister had possessed dark hair; his daughter had been crowned with red.

"Boleyn," he answered. "They always said there was another child. A boy. Born first and spirited away."

The pieces began to fall into place. Before King Henry had lost his mind over Anne Boleyn—leaving the church, changing England and religion forever—he had first sampled her sister.

Which had worked out well for him, as he could then use the former alliance with Mary—considered incestuous by the church he'd already renounced—as a means to get rid of Anne when he'd tired of her.

"You are saying that Prospero is the son of Mary Boleyn and King Henry?" I clarified.

"He does look very much like him."

Will should know.

"But . . . how came he here?" I asked.

"It matters not." Will strode past both Caliban and me. "What matters is that he is going after his throne, and the throne is that of our queen."

Chapter Forty

"To cry to the sea that roar'd to us, to sigh to the winds whose pity, sighing back again, did us but loving wrong."

—*The Tempest* (Act I, scene 2)

Ariel stood on the beach in the cove where she'd left the ships.

They were gone. She could not see even a hint of their sails upon the horizon.

The rattle of foot upon stone caused Ariel to glance over her shoulder. Her diamond, the vampire, and Ariel's love made their way down the steep rise. She should have transported them here, but she'd been . . .

She was not sure.

Ariel set her hands to her face, which upon sight of the empty cove had flared hot with an emotion she could not put a name to.

Jealousy caused a burning in her belly.

Lust a fiery heat somewhat lower.

Love produced a fire within her chest.

But the heat in her cheeks? That she did not understand.

The newcomers joined her on the sand, and Ariel turned to her diamond. "What means it when thy cheeks dost burn? I wouldst like to stick my head in the earth and hide there until it doth stop."

The diamond's gaze was focused upon the empty cove. "Shame," she said. "'Tis shame that makes the cheeks burn and gives one a desire to hide."

"Shame?" Ariel repeated.

"Guilt. Disgrace," Katherine continued. "Regret for something thou hast done."

Ariel turned her eyes to the empty waves. "Aye."

"Where are the ships?" Shakespeare asked.

The falling moon, still glowing and full, sparked off the finger Ariel pointed at the horizon. "They are gone."

"Bring them back!" Katherine ordered.

"Bring a storm," Caliban suggested.

"They are beyond the reach of any storm I might conjure." Ariel sighed, and the wind did answer in kind. "If I had the power to make them return, I would have made them stay away in the first place."

"How are they so far gone?" Shakespeare wondered. "'Tis not been that long since I lifted the dead."

"A spell," she began. "For speed. He must have found it in the—"

"Book," they finished as one.

"I suspect he needed to hurry lest they rot," Katherine said.

"Or you killed them," Shakespeare agreed.

"He did not know she was here," Ariel blurted.

"He did." Caliban hung his head. "I am sorry. The words tumbled off my overly long tongue by mistake."

"I think your tongue is just right," Ariel murmured, and her monster's head came back up. She smiled at him. "Things happen." Then her smile fell at another thought. "But if my master knew how I had attempted to thwart him, why did he release me?"

"In bringing a *chasseur* to the island, you also brought me," Shakespeare said. "And I gave him what he wanted. Mayhap he was feeling generous."

Ariel did not think her master knew the meaning of the word; she was, however, free.

"We must follow," Shakespeare said.

"Can you send us hence?" the diamond asked.

"Soon." Ariel shifted her gaze to the left, where the tip of a sail had just become visible. She sighed again, and the wind whistled.

"Might you tell us what you know of your master?" Shakespeare asked.

Ariel considered the vessel. 'Twould not be here for hours, and they had little else to pass the time.

"His mother was a witch," she said. "She could control the moon, make flows and ebbs. He inherited the talent from her, as well as the book."

"That explains how the moon became full when it should not be," Shakespeare murmured.

The diamond caught her breath, and Ariel cast her a sharp look. "Didst thou know such a woman?"

Katherine's lips tightened; her forehead did crease. "There were rumors of the present queen's mother. They say she bewitched the king and was beheaded for it."

"You think she didst have magic?"

"If she did, then why would she allow herself to be beheaded?"

The diamond spoke true. Anyone with power would find another way.

"Unless," Shakespeare said, "her power lay in a book, which was stolen by her sister."

Katherine's eyebrows lifted. "I had not thought of that."

"What sister?" Ariel asked.

"The miniature," Shakespeare began, and suddenly Ariel understood.

"My master's mother was the beheaded queen's sister."

"We think it may be so," Katherine said.

"Hmm." Ariel put her silver finger to her silver face. "I always thought he was lying."

"Or insane," Shakespeare muttered.

"Aye. He told me he was put here by a demi-devil, the servant of a bastard, because there were too many heirs."

"He *is* mad," her diamond said. "One thing of which the Tudors have always been in short supply is heirs."

"Which might be why he was stranded here and not killed." Shakespeare spread his hands. "A demi-devil? The servant of a bastard?"

Katherine gave a quick shake of her head. "I do not catch your meaning."

"Lord Burghley. William Cecil, the queen's closest adviser. He would do anything for her."

"The servant of a bastard," Katherine whispered.

"Do not let her, or him, hear you say that," Caliban muttered.

"Or I might find myself stranded upon a deserted isle," Katherine agreed. "I can almost understand Prospero's anger."

"Kate!" Shakespeare exclaimed. "She is our queen."

"And an excellent queen she is. But to be hidden then discarded. To fear for one's life every day is to invite madness."

"Elizabeth was both hidden and discarded," Shakespeare

said. "She spent the first twenty-odd years of her life in fear *for* her life, and she is far from mad."

"You are right." Katherine set her hand atop Shakespeare's. "Some come to greatness through adversity, and some find themselves crushed by it."

"We need to crush him." Shakespeare turned his gaze upon the western horizon.

"Thy chariot cometh," Ariel murmured.

All eyes turned toward the ever-expanding sail to the east.

Several hours later, Caliban emerged from the rushes where he had crouched when the sailors arrived with the longboat.

Ariel had remained upon the beach. Sailors were human and therefore could not see her. She had no reason to hide.

Instead she had spewed mad laughter from the sky— *Bwa-ha-ha-ha!*—causing both Shakespeare and Katherine to cast long-suffering glances in her direction as they climbed aboard.

Ariel did not want any humans stepping foot here again. If these put about that this place was haunted, and considering all the ships that had been lost in these waters she was surprised it hadn't been labeled so before, her foolish laughter would be well rewarded. She wanted only to remain on this isle forever.

Ariel turned toward Caliban. With him.

Her heart had merely beat before he came into her life. Now it beat for him. She was not sure why, but she was glad of it.

Mayhap their similarities had drawn them together. He had not been the best of men; she had not been the best of sprites. They had done evil, but they had not known any better. Together, they had learned otherwise.

"You could have gone with them," she murmured.

"Why?" He indicated the island with a dangerous sweep of his claw. "When everything I adore is right here?"

Something else they shared. Though neither of them had been born here, this island was home. No other place ever could be.

"Mayhap there is someone in that world who could mend you," Ariel said.

"Someone once told me . . ." His cool, blue eyes warmed as he moved in close, not touching, yet still she felt him everywhere.

Love, Ariel had discovered, was like that.

"There is nothing in need of repair."

Chapter Forty-one

"Our revels now are ended."

—*The Tempest* (Act IV, scene 1)

Will and Kate stood at the bow of the ship as the first faint tinge of England darkened the horizon.

"We'll stop them, Will." Kate set her hand upon his where it lay upon the rail. "We have done it before."

"Not this many." He swallowed thickly. "I am such a fool."

"We have all been fools for love."

Will had been much more than a fool. He'd raised a zombie army against his beloved queen, and he hadn't even gotten his life back. That bastard Prospero had sailed away without bothering to make Will human. Will was beginning to wonder if the man even could.

"You have forgiven me?"

Kate leaned her head against his shoulder. "Of course."

And with those words, Will knew he was blessed, even if he remained forever cursed.

"'Twas an interesting place," he said. "A beautiful isle, a sorcerer, a beast, and a fairy."

"Such stuff," she whispered, "as dreams are made on."

Will's skin prickled at her words. "Aye," he agreed. "Dreams."

"A play?" she asked, and he but smiled.

As often happened, Will's mind became occupied with his idea. Characters spoke. He spoke back. His fingers itched for a quill. When Kate kissed his cheek once more and went inside, he barely noticed she had gone.

"I will call it *The Storm*," he murmured, gazing upon the horizon, where what he had thought was the long low coastline of England had begun to whirl and billow like—

"Da tempest."

Nounou stood at his side, tall and regal, the ends of her multicolored headdress remaining still despite the sudden increase of the wind.

"Where have you been?" he asked.

"Dat island." Nounou shook her head; her headdress did not move. "'Twas Zombie Island. No room for any more dead."

Will kept his eyes on that odd, billowing cloud. He did not like it.

"Everything will be all right," Nounou said.

"The ships are full of the walking dead. What of England? The queen? And Prospero?"

"Dere is more to dis story."

Ghosts always knew the truth, and they liked to come and tell him. Why would Nounou be any different?

"Two sisters," she continued. "Both witches. One possesses a stolen book of spells."

Will's gaze narrowed. "Go on."

"Dis sister controlled de moon, de flows and ebbs. Her talent was passed to her firstborn."

"And the other?" Will turned again toward England, where

the sky had gone black and lightning had begun to flash most strangely.

"De other," Nounou murmured, "controlled de storm."

"The queen—" he began.

"She inherited de throne from her father, but de means to protect it . . ." Nounou smiled. "In dat she is her mother's child."

Will stared at the swirling, raging gale and understood that by the time they arrived, Queen Bess would have protected her country again as she had protected it at least once before.

"The Armada," he murmured.

Nounou chuckled. "Did you t'ink its destruction was an accident?"

Will hadn't thought; he'd merely been grateful for it.

No wonder the queen had barely blinked an eye when she'd discovered her favorite playwright was a vampire.

She was a witch!

THE BARD IS ALIVE!

"Handeland's foray onto the monster-lit stage deserves a standing ovation."—*LIBRARY JOURNAL*

"Fun...this bawdy send-up should slake the thirst of mash-up lovers."—*KIRKUS REVIEWS*

St. Martin's Griffin